Secrets

WALL STREET JOURNAL & USA TODAY BESTSELLING AUTHOR

SAPPHIRE KNIGHT

Copyright © 2015, 2016, 2017, 2018, 2019, 2020

Secrets by Sapphire Knight

Editing by Mitzi Carroll

This book is a work of fiction. The names, characters, places, and incidents are products of the writer's imagination or have been used fictitiously and are not to be construed as real. Any resemblance to persons, living or dead, actual events, locales or organizations is entirely coincidental.

All rights reserved. With the exception of quotes used in reviews, this book may not be reproduced or used in whole or in part by any means existing without written permission from the author.

The author acknowledges the trademarked status and trademark owners of various products referenced in this work of fiction, which have been used without permission. The publication/use of these trademarks is not authorized, associated with, or sponsored by the trademark owners.

WARNING

This novel includes graphic language and adult situations. It may be offensive to some readers and includes situations that may be hotspots for certain individuals. This book is intended for ages 18 and older due to some steamy spots. This work is fictional. The story is meant to entertain the reader and may not always be completely accurate. Any reproduction of these works without Author Sapphire Knight's written consent is pirating and will be punished to the fullest extent of the law.

- This book is fiction.
- The guys are over-the-top alphas.
- My men and women are nuts.
- This is not real.
- Don't steal my shit.
- Read for enjoyment.
- This is not your momma's cookbook.
- Easily offended people should not read this.
- Don't be a dick.
- Romance shaming is slut-shaming; don't be that asshole.

Dedication

Jr- For thinking I'm some famous Author. When in reality, I'm just another little fish, swimming in a great big ocean.

Jay- For always getting Momma her laptop and another soda. You have no idea just how important your job really is.

Common Terms

Красивая – (kraaseevee) Beautiful
Красота (Krasaaveetsa) - Beauty
Большой босс (Balshoy Shef) - Big Boss
Босс *(Shef)* - Boss
Брат *(Braat)* - Brother
Пончик *(Пончик)* - Donut
Отец *(Atyets)* - Father
Ебать (Poshyol) – Fuck
Маленькая (mallenkee) - Little
Бог, я хотел ебать Вы так плохо красоты *(Bawg, ya khatyets poshyol Vee так plawkha* Krasaaveetsa*)* - God, I want to fuck you so bad beauty
Я утверждаю, вы как шахта красоты навсегда *(YA praava vee как maya* Krasaaveetsa, *nafsegDA)* - I claim you as mine beauty forever
Шахта *(Maya)* - Mine
Мой брат *(Moy braat)* - My Brother
Жаркое *(zazhaareets)* - Roast
Russkaya Mafiya- Russian Mafia
Торт - Type of Russian dessert
Сестра *(Saystraa)* - Sister
Она является шахта *(Anaa maya)* - She is mine
Сын (sin) - Son
Корзина *(moosar)*- Trash
Да *(Da)* – Yes

Three sources were checked for the Russian Language. Formal spelling as well as pronunciation are included. It's meant to help with the setting, to draw you in and help you connect with the characters, it may not be 100% accurate, but this is **FICTION.**

Chapter 1

Emily

Deep breaths, Deep breaths, mm ah, mm ah.

Geez, I gotta relax before I give myself a panic attack. I can't believe I'm stuck starting at a new school and had to skip a semester of my sophomore year. Definitely is not what I had imagined looking into the future for myself.

University of Tennessee; I look around and can't help but feel some excitement. The scent of the freshly-cut campus lawns, bees buzzing happily, and big bushes of Knock Out roses adorn some of the corners along the sidewalks. The buildings are huge, making the many groups of people appear small. All this orange reminds me of home and makes me love it more.

No one knows who I am or anything about me and that gives me a sense of safety, finally. Not that I'll be out when it's dark, walk by any shadows or leave my windows open. I'm not completely stupid or oblivious to my own safety, even if I am far away. I have been known to be slightly naive, but do my best not to be.

I glance at the pink carbon copy of my schedule again. Ugh. I'm taking all my classes early in the morning. This way I don't have to be out in the evenings and it sucks, royally. I'm so not a morning person and to say I'm a little paranoid is extremely accurate.

First on the agenda is Government II. This should be interesting, or not. I'm definitely going to have to take major notes. I've always been pretty smart, but come on, History and Government? No way. Too boring for even the intelligent people.

I can seriously see this lecture going in one ear and out the other. Thank God for my Route 44 soda. One thing I love about the south is our many options for huge beverages.

Naturally, I make my way to sit in the back of the lecture hall. I really hope I can blend in unnoticed, and perhaps get an occasional nap in if needed. The room is huge with rows of plain, brown tables and standard chairs. There's a solid, black podium at the front of the room for the professor and an oversized whiteboard placed behind it, for easy use.

I'm sure my massive Styrofoam cup is like a white beacon in front of me, amongst these Starbucks drinkers. All this coffee-smelling air is making me miss my best friend, London. Missing London makes me miss home.

God, I wish I could be in Texas.

Hopefully one day I can go back to my granddaddy's land. I better call London's brother, Elliot, to make sure everything's going okay with him taking care of the house and land. I keep forgetting with everything going on. I never expected moving a few states would be so draining and stressful.

I'm brought out of my thoughts by a bright smile and chipper voice, "Hi! Boy, I hope this class doesn't suck, you know? It's so hard having a class this early that requires me to think. I'm Avery, nice to meet you," she babbles as she slides into the chair next to me.

I guess I'm no longer alone back here in my hermit-like world. I should have known potential nap time was too good to be true. I don't enjoy early conversation, but this pretty girl looks like she may talk my ear off regardless.

"Hi, I'm Emily." I shoot her a small smile. "Nice to meet you too, Avery." I normally love meeting new people, I'm just sleepy and it kind of makes me a grouch.

"Have you had Mr. Pottsmooth before?" She slides into the chair next to me, dumping her bag on top of the desk. "I haven't but I heard he can be tough if you don't study hard. But I *so* need this class, so what can you do, right?" Avery pulls out a hot pink notebook and a bright blue pen to go with it. "Oh! I know—we can be study partners, maybe it'll make this class a little fun?" She gazes at me with a hopeful look and I attempt to return it with a friendly expression.

I really don't know what to respond to at this moment. She just asked me like ten questions and I'm not even halfway through my soda yet. She seems really sweet though, maybe just nervous. Unless, perhaps Avery talks this much all of the time?

"No, I haven't had him before, either," I mumble and chew on my lip.

Saved! In walks Professor Humpty Dumpty by the looks of it. I can't help but snort a little to myself. He and his big belly are stuffed in a terry cloth track suit. I didn't even know they made those for men. Are they even allowed to wear that to work? I know this is college, but there has to be some type of dress code for instructors, surely.

Once that disaster of a lecture is over with, I'm cornered once again by Avery.

A cheeky smile graces her face as she talks way quicker than your average southerner, "Wow, definitely didn't see that one coming!" She gestures, talking with her hands, "Did you see what that man was wearing? And he totally talked monotone the whole class. I mean, who does that? Not raise your voice a decibel and talk through your nose the whole time." She starts giggling, thoroughly amused, and I have to chuckle along with her. Avery just has such a cheery bubble around her that pulls you in and she's kind of a silly mess.

"So Emily, I work at this great little coffee shop a few blocks away. It's called 'A Sip of Heaven,' cheesy, I know. Anyhow, wanna go have a cup and talk about all these stupid requirements for this class?"

"Sorry Avery, but I have to get to my other class. Maybe some other time we can meet for some ice cream or something?"

That's if she's even really serious about us being friends. A few people to hang out with here might make it more bearable with the amount of homework it seems I'm going to have. I need to surround myself with at least a few female friends.

"OH MY GAWD! I love ice cream! Okay, that sounds great!" She grabs my phone quickly and my eyes go wide. Geez, I thought I was going to drop it and that's the last thing I need.

Avery calls her phone before I even realize what she's up to and hands it back when hers rings with some rock song. "Okay, friend, program my number since you have it now and I'll text you later so we can meet up."

Just as quickly as she swooped in, she's off, bouncing down the hallway. I think I might really end up liking this girl a lot. If only we met after ten in the morning, I would have had much better conversation skills. Avery grins, waving happily as she makes her way down the large beige hallway and I wave back.

Thankfully, the rest of my day breezes through swiftly and with no drama. The lectures dragged a little, but that's pretty standard for the first classes. So far, Avery's the only person I've said more than a few words to. I didn't realize how lonely this would be, moving out here all alone, with no one knowing where I am. Well, minus London and her family.

I had to do it though. I had very little choice left if I wanted to be safe in the future. I'm going to keep on trekking through and just try to be grateful I have a chance to start fresh. I have to remind myself that I almost wasn't this lucky. I nearly wasn't able to get out. I thank my lucky stars daily for my momma watching over me and good people that helped me.

I wasn't expecting Avery to text me right away, but she did. She invited me out to eat and I have to say I'm pretty excited to meet her for dinner. I can handle being on my own the majority of the time but there is nothing worse than eating by yourself.

I hadn't even made it in the door of my apartment after classes without having three new text messages from her. Maybe I won't end up being too lonely after all, at least I hope not. Her cheery persona seems to just rub off and makes you want to surround yourself with that type of person. On top of that I didn't have much to remember from my first set of classes either. I'd say it was a good morning.

I don't have very much money to splurge on going out, but because of Granddaddy's life insurance he set up before he was taken from me, I'm able to eat out and not completely penny-pinch. Once I turned eighteen, I was able to access my momma's life insurance policy. My granddad never spent a cent, always saying it should be for when I was starting my own life without him. Thank God for his stubbornness and future planning or I wouldn't be here in Tennessee right now.

Avery invited me to a bar and grill called 'The Flamingo Grill.' I had never heard of it but promised to meet her. Wherever doesn't matter as long as it's close to my apartment. I'm not looking to get lost just yet. This city is overwhelming as it is.

My granddaddy's teal, 1965 Ford F100 pickup truck he left me when he passed doesn't have GPS. She drives like a dream and I couldn't imagine driving something other than this beauty. This girl might be a classic, but thankfully, in this heat, her air conditioner works like she's brand new.

I didn't realize Tennessee was going to be more humid than Texas when I packed up and moved out here. Hello muggy afternoon. I know it could be plenty worse; at least I have the right clothes. I could be stuck up north, freezing my tush off.

I take extra care sorting through my tiny closet, picking out which sundress and boots I'm planning on wearing this evening. For my usual attire, I'll just throw on the first one I come across. I really want to look nice today; I have no idea what the dress code is for this place. Shoot, in Texas a sundress and boots works wherever you go, so that is pretty much what my closet is full of.

Sifting through the many colors, I pick a pale yellow that's one of my favorites. It falls over me perfectly and it still looks new enough to wear out to eat in. The dress stops above my knees tastefully and my brown cowboy boots that have a pretty 'choker' on each, completes my outfit nicely.

I throw on some Clinique Lash Doubling mascara in black. Then twist a few curls in my long, dirty blonde hair with my curling iron, and boom! I'm all set. I may not be runway ready, but this will definitely work for dinner.

As it turns out, The Flamingo is not that hard to find with its giant pink fake bird on the roof. Avery's sweet face is out front waiting for me when I pull into the lot. I park away from other vehicles. I can't have my baby girl getting scratched up from other people's negligence. Granddaddy would be turning in his grave if he saw me park too close.

"Hey, girl!" I holler and wave at Avery as soon as I open my door.

I give her a big smile as I walk toward her, weaving in between cars. There are two other rows of cars parked in front of my truck in the large parking lot. The place looks pretty busy as most of the spots are filled. Hopefully a lot of the vehicles belong to employees; I would hate it if there's a wait to be seated.

Avery meets me as soon as I step on the sidewalk near the front entrance. "Hey, Emily! Geez, you look so cute! I love your dress!" She grabs my hand while talking superfast, all excited like.

We make our way closer to the entrance and she leans in to talk lower for my ears only, "I hope you don't mind, but I ran into a couple of guys from one of my classes and they asked if we wanted to sit together. They are totally hot so of course I told them yes. I hope you don't mind. Girl, you are gonna be happy when you see these fine men!" She flashes me a brilliant smile after and I roll my eyes.

"Okay, Avery, but I'm not really looking to meet any guys. I'm just here to concentrate on school."

I am so not ready for another relationship. My life is way too complicated right now as it is. I know college guys are going to be after one thing anyhow and I'm for sure not looking for a hook up.

"Emily, you have to relax a little or you'll get burned out and we have barely bitten into this semester." She chastises me as we head towards two really good-looking guys, waiting inside by the hostess station. "Okay, here we are! Miss Emily, this is Cameron Wentworth and Luka Masterson." She gestures towards them with her hand as if she's presenting some sort of prize.

I flash them a nervous little grin and wave my hand like a dork. Cameron is cute in that rich preppy jock style.

Clearing my throat, I mumble, "Hi, Cameron, nice to meet you."

"Hey, Emily, you too." He shoots me his bright white smile that I'm sure gets all the girls excited. I've seen his kind before and avoid them like the plague. I remember the jock types in high school, always floating around messing with as many girls as possible.

I look over to Luka and it's like a punch to the gut. He's freaking beautiful, like should be posing in a magazine type of good-looking. "Umm... Hi, Luka," I choke out.

Thank fuck I didn't stutter, sweet Jesus. I hope to God my mouth is shut right now and I'm not gawking like an idiot. I'm met with the most striking hazel eyes when I look up and I have to look up, this man is definitely pushing six foot-two or six foot-three.

"Hey, Emily, please call me Tate." His voice is smooth and rich like honey. The kind of voice that vibrates through your bones and wraps you up to make you feel warm inside. I love his name. You don't hear 'Tate' often. It suits him.

He reaches for my hand and when he touches me, I feel squiggles in my belly. I gasp in an almost silent breath. I hope he doesn't notice my reaction to him. This is the type of man that could steal me, own me and eventually break me. I'm already too broken as it is.

The tall, thin hostess leads us to our booth after a few brief moments of her collecting menus and wrapped silverware for us. I happily follow her through the main entry and around the bar. We got lucky not having to really wait. I know some restaurants around colleges have an hour or so wait time. I almost want to slip her a five for breaking up the awkward first

11

impression, I'm sure I gave. However I doubt she noticed, since she was busy gawking at the guys.

We each slide in and she passes the menus to us, giving a spiel about our server and daily specials. The booth isn't too large, but we aren't exactly crammed in either. We have just enough room to feel the warmth of the person next to us. The tables are a shiny oak surrounded by rich, red leather covered booths.

Once we all settle in, I feel like a big nerd just staring. I can't help it though. Men shouldn't be allowed to be this good looking. It's not fair to the female population; we already have to grow up realizing we can't all be princesses, and then life throws genes like this at us.

Tate is nicely built. He doesn't have that steroid bulk build like some of the men around campus I saw today, but he's in great shape. He has really short, dark brown hair. I could easily run my fingers through it. You know if I was looking to do that sort of thing, but I'm not. I can still daydream though. *Gosh, I bet it's really soft.*

Cameron is pretty cute himself. He's a few inches shorter than Tate but still easily towers over Avery and me. He's blessed with sandy blond hair, longer than Tate's and each time he grins, his chocolate brown eyes sparkle. The two of them together probably have to push the girls off each other with a stick.

Glancing at Tate, I attempt for some easy conversation, "Hey Tate, it sounds like you have a little bit of an accent. What is it?"

His eyes shine playfully as he gazes at me, "That's rich, coming from a sweet southern thing. You've got quite the twang yourself, sweetie."

I don't know if he is being a condescending dick to me or just taking the attention from my question to his comment. Regardless, I huff and keep quiet. I generally keep to myself until I know someone well anyhow. I just can't help myself from talking to him, it's like he sucks up all of the attention. This is good though, if I'm angry at him at least I won't be picturing his abs every time he speaks to me.

Thankfully, the server approaches to take our orders. Avery and Cameron dominate most of the conversation, so I can just sit back and watch Tate. It feels like I'm in a fuzzy dream, as my body hums with nerves. I don't want to stick my foot in my mouth and I don't really want to reveal much. I have to lie low and keep to myself. I need to be careful about too many people getting to know me. I hate having to make all new friends.

"Excuse me for a moment," I mumble, sliding out of the booth and heading for the bathroom. It'll give me a few moments to catch my bearings and pull myself together.

I come back from the restroom feeling a little more confident from the sporadic pep talk I gave myself in the women's stall to see Tate laughing. *God, he is handsome.* His laugh is deep and his eyes flicker with humor, it's like a vacuum pulling me to him. I can't help but wonder if I could make him smile and laugh that way.

I concentrate on eating my oversized baked potato that's loaded to the brim with butter, sour cream, cheese and bacon. It's delicious and I shovel it down quickly. With Granddad you learned to eat swiftly or you went hungry. He was in the military when he was young and has always been a fast eater.

I'm brought out of my brain freeze from my virgin Pina Colada I was busily sucking down by Avery's chipper voice, "Hey Emily, you ready to go?" She leans into me and bumps me with her elbow lightly, "These two kind gentlemen refuse to let us pay for our meals. Isn't that sweet?"

Avery is looking way too happy about this. Personally, I don't want to owe anybody anything, but this time I'm just going to act like it doesn't bother me. I leave the cool, sweet trance I was in with my beverage and smirk at the guys.

"Yep, I'm ready. And thank you, this is so kind of you to treat us to dinner. We owe you guys." I regret the words instantly. *Dumb ass.* I scold myself and shake my head a little. Just great, these guys probably think I'm a nut job.

"Well, speaking of owing, how about you give me your number? I might have trouble in a few of my classes and need your help someday." Tate's eyes gleam mischievously and I have to bite back my groan. Geez, did I not just say I didn't want to owe anybody anything? I guess this is better than a date or him wanting me to wash his car or something. Plus, I can always block his number if I need to.

Shrugging I say irritably, "Sure, if it's for help, then no problem, but I'm definitely no booty call," I say in my snarkiest voice possible. Maybe he'll change his mind.

Cameron laughs and chortles out, ribbing Tate, "Oh, boom! Man, she put you in your place!"

Cameron looks like he just won the lottery and I'm his new best friend. I roll my eyes and turn my head away. Why do men have to act like jackasses sometimes?

"Shut your face Cameron, and no Emily, I am very aware you are not the type of girl to be just a random booty call. Trust me, I have plenty of females for just that purpose. Babe, you would know if you were going to be my booty call." He appears sincere and I don't know if that's a compliment or not, but at least we're on the same page.

We all trade numbers; Avery and Cameron way more enthusiastic than Tate and me. I think he may finally be getting it that I am not interested in him. It's probably a shock to his system, but I've had my fill of men to last awhile.

Avery and I thank the boys again for dinner. My southern manners drilled into me, almost makes it impossible for me to be mean to people. They insist on walking us to our vehicles. I agree grouchily. I may appear bitchy to them but it's on purpose. I don't want to give anyone the wrong impression and some men just don't get it when things are spelled out plain as day.

Avery doesn't have a vehicle so Cameron offers to give her a ride in his little Porsche. If I would have known that before I would have offered for us to ride here together. It would be nice to have someone who knows where exactly they are going. Judging by the look radiating on her face, I know I am going to hear all about it later. She is practically glowing.

"Thanks for inviting me, Avery; I'll see you in class," I hug Avery and then high-five Cameron. "Bye, Cameron."

"Anytime, sweet cheeks, text me later!" She calls as they walk off. Avery is probably going to bounce out of her shoes; she's vibrating with so much excitement. *Yep, definitely going to hear about that!*

I quickly head to my truck parked all by its lonesome. It's a little spooky out here at nighttime, even with the night air whispering with the songs playing from the restaurant's outdoor speakers.

The air has cooled slightly but still feels thick. The bugs make crazy sounds, providing the illusion of the country, when in fact it's a busy city.

We make it to my truck and sense of comfort washes over me, just from being near something so familiar. "Thank you for walking me to my truck, Tate," I murmur gratefully.

I look around and take in my surroundings. The parking lot isn't packed, but there are quite a few cars. I'm always scanning for a certain face. I'm glad I don't have to walk to the truck by myself, I'd probably freak myself out and drop my keys.

"Hey, no problem. Wow! Nice ride, never pictured you in something like this."

"It was my granddad's. He built it all himself and gave it to me."

I smile fondly at her blue-green shimmer from the streetlamps. I would trade this truck in a heartbeat, just to have him back. I miss him every single day. My chest always gets tight when I think of him, the man who took care of me for so long. Now I'm left without him, to make it on my own.

"Lucky girl. Hey, I meant what I said back there. I know you're not a booty call. You are way too sweet and beautiful to be mistaken as trashy." He gazes at me seriously. "Would you mind if I text you later though?" I stare at him for a beat and I think he looks like he's being pretty sincere, so why not.

15

"Okay you can text me," I reply without hesitation. "Good night, Tate." I smile slightly and look up into his hazel eyes.

I'm such a wimp. I put up no fight whatsoever. At this point he could ask for a back rub and I'd probably ask if he wanted lotion too. I'm sure this is how he starts with all females. He comes off as just wanting to be friends and then swoops in when they're least expecting it.

"Good night, *Krasaaveetsa.* (Beauty)"

He leans into me and gives me a small hug. He smells so good; crisp and clean. His body is warm, and even in the small amount of contact we make I can feel him. He presses his full lips softly to my forehead and I melt.

For the first time in forever I feel safe.

Chapter 2

I'm roused out of my sleep by the ding of an incoming text. I sent London's brother, Elliot, a text last night, asking how the house was doing. He never replied back, but that's probably him now.

I poke my arm out of my comforter, flailing my hand around on my nightstand. I blindly search for my phone; I could open my eyes and actually look for it, but that would be too easy. It's nippy in here so I'm going to try to stay as covered up as possible.

My eyes bug out when I see it's in fact from Tate and not Elliot Traverson.

Tate Masterson – Good morning, Красота

Wow, I wasn't expecting him to text me. It's been two days since we had dinner. I thought guys were supposed to wait like three days to a week so they don't seem eager?

Okay, I have to break down and ask him what this name means. I have literally been thinking of it nonstop the past few days since I heard him say it. I wasn't sure exactly how I heard it pronounced or how it's spelled, or else I would have Googled it already.

Me – Hi, what does that mean?

Tate Masterson – What does what mean?

Me – You know! Красота?

Tate Masterson – It means pop tart.

Giggling, I flap the covers down to poke my head out. He has my heart racing excitedly and I know I won't be able to drift off to sleep again. I blink rapidly a couple times to clear my eyes and quickly type back.

Me – Pop tart! Seriously?

Tate Masterson – LOL! Have a good day, sweet Emily...

Me – I will figure it out! You too!

I can't help the beaming smile I have after our short conversation. It's been a really long time since someone has kind of flirted with me. Wait was that flirting? I think it was. My stomach flips, feeling a little giddy that he texted me after all.

Now I need soda, some clothes and then I'm off to class again. This early morning crap is for the birds. I reach under my small bed to find my twenty-four pack of Coca-Cola and pop one open. I take the first refreshing drink before my feet even hit the floor. The little zip of caffeine always helps me prepare for the day.

I brush my hair and blow-dry it slightly to get some creases out. Every time I sleep with it wet, I wake up looking like some crazed maniac. I go with a cute pink sundress, since I'm already in a happy mood. Pairing the dress with some tan wedges, since I'm barely pushing five foot-three inches, my look is complete. The shoes are the perfect help I need in the height department!

I grab my drink and backpack on my way out the door. I hope I didn't forget anything. I know my notes and stuff are in my bag, but I still get nervous. The college I came from was a little more laid back, so I'm trying to stay on my toes.

I make my way to building 119 for my Biology course with no issues, thankfully. I really enjoy the walk over even if I am slightly paranoid. I'm still a little scatterbrained with this new school. I had printed out the school map before I started and studied it countless times.

The green lawns of the university are so plush looking, I bet it would be comfortable to lie on and read a good book. I love how the sidewalks are lined with trees. They provide the perfect canopy of shade to escape some of the heat. Now if only there was a cool breeze to compliment it all.

I get into the stuffy Biology classroom and make my way down the aisle between the desks. I weave through until I find the perfect spot. I hate sitting with people to my back, but I know I have to be able to hear in order to pass this class. I just pray I don't end up having to dissect any creatures. That will be my breaking point.

A deep voice attempts to catch my attention but I stare straight ahead, attempting to ignore him, "Pst... Hey... Pst... Hey, Hey!"

OMG, it is way too early for any idiot to try to talk to me. After a few times, I glance back out of the corner of my eye. I don't want to give them my full attention and egg them on.

I'm met with blond hair and a sweet smirk. *Oh! It's Cameron!* He's sitting behind me, leaning his chair back on two legs.

"Hey, Cameron. You're going to hurt yourself!" I shake my head, chastising him. "I didn't see you when I came in or I would have said hello."

He's wearing his signature polo shirt; however, today it's in a different shade of grey. His white ball cap is pulled down low over his blood shot eyes and he looks exhausted. I bet if he stood up he'd be in khaki shorts.

He smirks, murmuring, "Hey, Goldilocks! It's cool, come sit by me."

He didn't seem so bad at dinner, so what the hell, why not. I pack my belongings back into my backpack and move beside him, attempting to quickly get resituated for this lecture. Surely this man won't talk as much as Avery does this early. He looks way too tuckered out for any meaningful conversation.

I scan the lecture hall and take in each of my classmates. I gaze at each face carefully, cataloging their features. *He's not here, you're safe.*

"Gosh, I hope I do okay in this class." I turn to him and smile a fake smile. No need for everyone to figure out I'm paranoid.

"Yeah, no kidding. Why do you think I asked you to sit by me?"

I start snickering a little until I hear a throat clear. A shadow falls over my desk and I look up. I stare straight into Luka 'Tate' Masterson's pissed-off hazel glare. God, he's even hotter when he looks mad. His cheeks flush slightly and he screams alpha.

"Well, good morning, sunshine!" I croon in the cheeriest voice I can, smiling brightly.

Tate looks fantastic today in a pair of nice-fitting jeans leading past his muscular thighs to some black Polo boots. He has the top of his black button-up shirt unbuttoned with the sleeves rolled up. *Look at those tattoos.* I didn't see them the other night at dinner. Who would have guessed this rich boy could pull off tattoo sleeves. I can't really make out what they are, but holy hotness, they make him look even sexier. He has that 'I'm a bad boy, don't fuck with me' look, going today.

Ugh, we all know I like them bad, too. With that thought, I cringe a little.

"Enjoying yourself with Wentworth, I see," he grumbles out. "Can I join you or is this a private party?" he huffs. Yep, definitely has the asshole gene. Geez, did he just growl at Cameron?

"Of course, you're welcome to sit here. You're also welcome to get some coffee or whatever you need before you come next time."

"Oh, baby, I don't need coffee to come. Your sweet smile will do just fine," he replies cockily and licks his lips.

"Seriously, Tate? I'm just going to move."

I glare at him, disgusted. I know I must be tomato red right now. I don't have time for this shit. Who does he think he is, talking to me like that?

"I'm really sorry *Krasaaveetsa* (Beauty). Forget I just said that. Stay, I'll behave, promise."

I roll my eyes and nod, irritated. Cameron scoots his chair over so Tate can sit in between us. I don't know why he didn't just sit on the other side of Cameron. I don't plan on talking to him, especially after that loser line. I was so excited about that text earlier, too.

Tate fist bumps Cameron, and then he puffs his yummy plump bottom lip out towards me. He tries to look sorry and innocent, but it just annoys me further. *I just want to bite that lip.* Holy shit, did I really just think that? No.

No biting for me, focus. Think Biology, not man hunk with an accent. Is that Russian? I think that just raised his hotness factor even more. I am such a freaking goner.

I turn away from him and do my best to pay attention to the professor. Tate keeps brushing his arm against me, causing little goosebumps to erupt on my skin. I know he's doing it on purpose and I just want to kick him for it. I refuse to give in and look at him. This is going to be the longest class of my life.

I keep going back to the accent. Fuck, that's hot! Not only do I have to sit next to this absolutely gorgeous guy, but I have to smell him, too. He smells as good as he did last night at dinner. I think he's wearing Hugo Boss cologne. It's one of my favorites on a guy and it kind of makes me want to sit on his lap and sniff him everywhere. Maybe even lick his cheek at this point; I bet he tastes like a fine chocolate caramel candy. *Asshole.*

I didn't hear a word the professor said during that lecture. I stuff my things back into my bag quickly, pretending I'm in a super big hurry to get to my next class. After the longest two hours ever, I skirt out of class quickly and I give a quick "See ya," to no one in general.

I wave on my way out the door and practically run down the long hallway. I'm so glad my next class is pretty close by. I kind of expected Tate to follow me, but he didn't.

Neither Tate nor Cameron is in my next class so I can keep to myself like a hermit. I tuck back towards the rear of the room and pull my phone out. I may as well relax a little now that my body doesn't feel like it's vibrating any longer.

I sign onto London's Facebook page to troll around some. I don't have one really, so I share hers. What are best friends for, right? No one has posted anything about any jail release so I can take a deep calming breath. Another day, I don't have to worry about him finding me.

I definitely need a cool shower when I get out of class and a new pair of panties after that run in with Tate. My Facebook disappears when my phone flashes a new text from Avery. Still nothing from Elliot; I wonder if that punk got a new girlfriend or something. He's normally pretty quick to text me back.

Avery – Hey, chick! You should stop by the shop when you're done with class and visit me.

Me – Hi Avery! Do you have anything besides coffee and tea there?

Avery – Yes ma'am, hot chocolate.

Me – Oh! I LOVE hot chocolate! Okay, sounds like a plan. See you in about 20.

Avery – Awesomesauce!

I huff out a small laugh to myself. I know she's jumping up and down right now. That girl has so much energy all the time. Like a big happy bubble. I'm so lucky to have met someone like her so quickly.

I have to keep reminding myself to be careful. I wish I could just be happy and free like Avery. I don't know if I'll ever get to live without looking over my shoulder. I gaze at the girls hanging around campus—all so carefree—on the way to my truck. These chicks have no idea how easy they have it. Never having to worry about who could be following them, finding them, or hurting them.

That reminds me, I need to call London and see if she's heard anything about *him*. I know she said she would text but I have to make sure he's still in jail. London's been my best friend since we were five years old and started kindergarten. I know I can trust her but I just have this weird feeling. I'm probably overreacting but I can't let him find me. I can't go through that again.

God, I miss home. I wish I could feel the sweet Texas air on my granddaddy's land, softly kissing my skin. I love to just lie in the grass and look up at the beautiful stars. I want to be able to stroke my horse Thunder's soft mane and tell him everything that I'm thinking of. Just like I always have in the past.

I want to go home. No, this is home now. I have to learn to love Tennessee. I don't know if I'll ever get to go back to Texas again.

With that sad thought, I pull open the door to A Sip of Heaven. Drawing in a deep breath, I paste a big, fat, fake smile on my face. My mask.

Standing behind the dark green counter, Avery beams a cheerful, bright smile in my direction as I come in the door. "Hey, pretty little Emily! How's it going?" I think Avery must be the most content person I know. She is literally happy and smiling every single time I see her. I envy her so much.

"Hi, it's going okay, glad to be out of that boring-ass class, that's for sure! How's work?"

Avery has on her cute little apron and matching green polo shirt. She's the picture-perfect coffee shop employee today. She has her pretty, wavy, brownish hair tied up in a high ponytail. Adorable little silver coffee cup earrings dangle from her ears and bright pink painted nails.

Shrugging, she eyes me curiously, "Eh, its fine, kind of boring. Although I did see a hot man hunk, by the name of Cameron Wentworth and his dark haired god of a best friend, Luka Masterson. They mentioned something about a saucy little blonde yelling at Luka, that he needed coffee," she giggles uncontrollably and I wince. "Know anything about that?"

"Oh My God, shoot me now!" I place my head in my hands and prepare to defend myself, "I did not yell at him! He was being a total grouch when I was talking to Cameron in class today. That was like right after he sent me a sweet text this morning, too. Men are so confusing."

Ugh, I know my face is red. What a bum, telling on me! I'm so going to give him a hard time when I see him again. That tattletale!

Avery gasps excitedly, "He texted you? Spill it!" I swear her smile just doubled in size and she has this mischievous look in her eyes. I bet the faker already knows everything. She and Cameron probably spent the afternoon gossiping like a group of high school girls.

"Umm, yeah, he might have just said good morning." I shrug the question off and go sit at a table as quick as I can. I know she's up to something just by one look.

"Oh no, you don't get to escape!" She follows, eyebrows raised, "Tell me about this text."

I smirk and check my phone. There's still no text from Elliot.

I chuckle and roll my eyes, "It was nothing. He just said good morning and told me I look like a pop tart."

"He actually said, by the way you look like a pop tart?" She's studying me like I've lost my mind.

"Well, no, he calls me this name in a weird language. I asked what it meant and he told me pop tart. I think he was just being silly though."

"Holy shit! Tate totally likes you! I freaking knew it when I saw him watch you walk to the bathroom at dinner. He was staring at you like you were a piece of cake he wanted to eat!" Hmm, he's the one who looks as good as a big piece of chocolate cake.

"No way, I think you were imagining things, he was kind of an ass to me at dinner. Especially about the whole accent thing. I mean, deflect much?"

I'm over this conversation. Yes, he's hot. No, I don't need to get anyone else involved with my drama and issues. God forbid if the *Monster* ever finds me, what he'll do to me if I'm with another guy. I shudder and then rub my arms to play it off like I just got a chill.

"Okay girly, you think what you want to!" Avery calls out in a singsong voice while she walks to the counter to serve customers.

I guess it's time for me to finish this hot chocolate and get out of here. I have a ton of work to do, thanks to having to go full-time to maintain my scholarship. I do love the school though, the buildings and the surroundings, it's all so charming. The humidity is great on my skin and hair, too.

I head up to the counter, gesturing to Avery. She meets me by the register. "Emily, would you like a snack or anything, too?"

I shake my head and send her a small smile. "No. Thanks for the drink, Avery. I have to head out to work on some homework. I'll text you soon though. Have fun working!"

She throws her arm up and waves behind her as she hurries to help another customer. "Okay, bye, chickadee!" Avery responds busily, concentrating on making some kind of coffee creation so she doesn't see me return her wave.

* * *

Picking my head up off my folded arms on my desk, I blink a few times trying to wake up. *Shit, what time is it?* I must have fallen asleep reading my book. I glance around groggily and notice my phone blinking.

I rub my hands over my face a few times. Oh man, I forgot to call London, too. I probably look like a loon. I have every single light on in my little apartment, all the drapes and blinds closed and a chair propped up against my front door. *Straight nut job,* I think, and then shake my head. I push the button to illuminate my screen and see it's a text from Avery with a picture attached showing a man's butt in jeans.

Avery – Look who I saw again!

This girl is crazy. I check the clock on my phone. Ten p.m. Holy cow, I slept for hours! Great, I won't be able to go back to bed now.

I close my textbooks and neatly stack them on the corner of my little black desk I got at Walmart. I place each notebook and folder next to its matching textbook. *There, nice and organized.*

Me – You are so silly, Avery, who on earth is the poor man you took pictures of?

I chuckle as I text her back. What a goofball. I wouldn't be surprised if she got the guy to let her take it willingly either.

25

Avery – Your future ex-boyfriend! Luka Masterson!

Me – You dork! And he said to call him Tate. I can't believe you took a picture of his butt! Did he see you?

This man obviously works out. I will definitely be saving this picture to my phone so I can look at it again in the future. I may not want to hook up with the guy, but I can definitely appreciate looking at him sometimes. Maybe she'll get one with his shirt off that I can keep, too.

Avery – He knows I took it. He said I had to send it to you if I wanted to keep it. Told you Tate likes you!

Me – OMG! You are fired!

Avery – LOL! Get dressed I'm coming to get you

Me – No way, you don't even know where I live! :D

Avery – 1900 Adams Apt 13. I'll be there in 20, get something sexy on, cause we are going out.

Me – WHAT? How do you know where I live?

Avery – 19 minutes and I'm dragging your butt out for some fun.

Shit! She's serious. Okay, I am so not wearing anything sexy, I don't want any extra attention drawn to me and I know Avery will get plenty of attention by herself. What to wear?

Cute little black dress and some hot pink stilettos? Yes, please. It's fast, easy and I love my pink shoes.

I'm going to put on a little darker makeup than my norm, and wear my hair down. Hopefully, I'll just blend in with the background behind Avery. I've got to remember to not let her post any Facebook pictures of us. That could turn into a train wreck. I have to be careful and any pictures online is way too much of a risk.

He's found me before when I've tried to leave. I can't let him find me again. With that thought, I top my look off with some pin-up girl red lipstick and open my door.

Right into Tate Masterson's waiting smile. Ahhh! What's he doing here?

Sapphire Knight

Chapter 3

Tate's eyes widen and his irises grow dark, as he looks me up and down. My heart speeds up as soon as I catch his scent. I draw in a deep breath, my mind going a million miles an hour.

I can't help but to feel completely blindsided. I'm going to strangle Avery! I can't believe she didn't tell me that Tate was coming. I would have pretended I was still asleep had I known.

Tate's changed his clothes since class. Now he has on a fitted white V-neck that clearly outlines his muscles and his tattoos are on full display. Light wash blue jeans hang deliciously from his hips, and I know from that picture they look amazing from the backside also. *God, he looks amazing.*

Tate leans in close, overtaking my space. His nearness startles me and forces me to back up against my door. I can't let Tate get any closer or else I will more than likely drag him inside my apartment.

I sputter out, breathless, "Tate? What are you doing here? I was just about to leave with Avery."

He grunts, leaning slightly closer to my face, "Yeah, she's with us, I came up to get you. Do you have a coat or something to cover up with?"

Tate keeps glancing at my shoulders and legs disconcerted. I know he's talking to me, but all I can think of is, God the stubble on his cheeks makes him look fantastic. Luckily he can't read my mind.

"To cover up with? Did it get cold outside?" I'm confused, it was so hot earlier.

"It's decent out, but you're showing a lot of skin with that dress on. Maybe you should wear some pants?" He suggests while raising his eyebrow.

Tate crosses his arms across his chest, causing his shirt to stretch as his muscles bulge. I don't know if it's supposed to intimidate me to change or what. It's definitely not going to work. I can't believe the nerve of this man and his caveman tactics. First, it was the growling and now he's telling me what to wear. If I wanted to be controlled, I would have stayed with my psycho ex.

"You are so not telling me what to wear. I'm dressed already and this is what I'm wearing." I declare sternly, "I'm meeting Avery, not you. Even if it was you, I still would not go and change!" I place my hand on his chest to give him a little shove away from me. When I make contact with his pecs, his nostrils flare. He glares heatedly down at me, as if I'm dinner.

"Let's just go. Avery and Cameron are waiting in the car." He growls out suddenly, looking pissed when he turns away and stomps down the hall.

Geez, is this man always so broody? I thought I was too serious all the time; clearly Tate has me beat. What on Earth could possibly be so bad in his life? Tate's beyond gorgeous, has money out the yin yang and appears to be somewhat intelligent. I swear I'll never understand men.

I trail behind him and when we get outside, I see a blacked out, lifted Tahoe with beefy tires parked at the curb. I wouldn't have guessed in a million years that Tate would drive something like this. He just earned some cool points with his choice of vehicle. Most of the guys from where I'm from have lifted trucks on big tires.

"What happened to your Mercedes you were in the other night?"

I've been told by London that I'm a very inquisitive person. I, however, tell her I have special snooping privileges with her since she's my best friend. Maybe she's right, I am nosey. I'll never admit it to her, though.

Tate glances back at me with a huff and opens the passenger door for me to get in. "I drove the SUV because I wanted you to be comfortable with the extra room."

I get in and his comment floors me. Tate was thinking about me when he picked out which vehicle to drive? That means he had already planned to see me tonight. If he was thinking about me though, then why did he have to go and be an ass to me about my damn clothes? Ugh, God this man is so confusing!

Avery leans forward, tapping me playfully on my shoulder, "Emily! Damn girl, you look hot! I see Tate found your place without any problems." She looks entirely too pleased with herself and it makes me want to throw something at her.

I smirk, "Glad someone appreciates my outfit, Tate wanted me to go back and change." I shoot him a smug look. Take that, big boy!

Cameron starts chuckling until Tate glares at him in the rearview mirror. He starts driving and doesn't say anything for a while. I can hear Avery and Cameron talking low with Avery fake giggling at random things. *Yeah, they are so going to fuck, if they haven't already.*

I'll admit I'm a little jealous. I wish I could get with a guy and not worry about all the complications. Perhaps I should have a one-night stand? It's okay to scratch the itch, and then send them home, right? Guys do it all the time, so why can't I? I think that would be a safer option for me. No possible crazy boyfriend or posting photos of us, that sort of thing.

Maybe that's what I'll do tonight. I'll see if there's anybody worth having a one-night stand with. The idea sounds ludicrous really, since I've never done that sort of thing before. I know Tate will be preoccupied, most likely with multiple women. I can't blame them though, he is so handsome. Obviously, Cameron and Avery are getting close, so I'm going to try to have some fun tonight.

"So where exactly are we going anyhow?"

I've been pretty much nowhere since I moved here. The most I've seen of Tennessee so far was the highway, the rest stops I made to get here and the surrounding lakes. The drive was beautiful, lots of trees and grassy hills. The road through Arkansas was absolutely horrible, all the bumps and dips. Thank God it was a quick drive through it or I would have gone nuts.

Avery leans forward between the seats, right when I turn to look into the back seat. She gets so close we almost butt foreheads and I jerk back. She laughs and I grumble. Crazy girl scared the shit out of me!

"We, my friend, are going to OO7. It's my favorite club in the whole wide world! We are going to get our drink on, dance on and our freak on!" She smiles manically and I grin back.

"What is this, are we stepping into a James Bond flick?" I inquire, curiously. They all chuckle around me, and I peer at everyone inquisitively for some answers.

Avery happily chortles out, "Oh no! I want to see your reaction when we walk in. You will just have to wait and see. Geez, their martinis are out of this world! We are going to shake our booties until our feet feel like they want to fall off!" She seems to always know exactly what to say to bring a smile to my face.

"Girl, you are such a dork! I'll dance, but no drinking for me."

I never know when I might need all my senses intact. I know one day he's going to be waiting for me in a dark parking lot. Keeping alert could save my life if I'm ever in that position.

"What?! We have two good-looking men who are more than capable to carry our asses out of there if needed. You are getting toasted, Emily!"

I've learned the hard way not to rely on men, I'm not about to start now. I shake my head minutely, "I'll dance, but no drinks for me."

"We will see!" Avery sings, and plops back. She is pretty much sitting on top of Cameron. He looks thrilled about it though, so whatever, none of my business.

Tate glances over at me and does that one-arm extended thing, men do when they drive. God, he's absolutely delectable right now, all serious. His forehead does this little crinkle thing like he's thinking about something really hard, then he shakes his head and faces forward again.

"Huh? What was that just now?"

"Nothing," he mumbles.

Nothing my ass! "Umm, no! You just did a little head shake thingy."

"Just stay close in the club, okay? There will be a lot of people there you don't know, and I don't want you getting lost."

Christ, this man. "Seriously? I'm twenty years old, Tate, and believe it or not, I am a grown woman. This is not the first time I've been to a club." Perhaps I just tie a rope to his belt buckle at this point?

"I'm very aware you are a grown woman, *Krasaaveetsa* (beauty). Just trust me, please," Tate grumbles. After a moment he relaxes his features and stares at me wearily.

"Okay stud, since you asked nicely. I guess I'll stick close. But if you start getting overly bossy, I'm gone."

Turning, I watch out of my window as we drive. There is only so much Luka 'Tate' Masterson I can take. He's so handsome, and then he opens his mouth and ruins it.

I think I'm going to call the bossy ass side 'Luka' and the sweet man hunk side 'Tate'. That makes it's easier to break up the two personalities. Shit, what if he's a narcissist or something? That would be my luck, entice yet another psycho. Well, if I did appeal to him. I don't think he's that interested though. He's made it clear he doesn't see me in the booty call picture, so maybe he's not attracted to me?

I burst out, quickly before I have a chance to think it through, "Do you have a personality disorder?" I gaze at him curiously. The people with personality disorders will admit it, right?

Tate glares, fuming for a few beats before he growls, "Fuck! I'm just going to drive, okay?"

Man, he looks pissed. Yep, he could totally have a personality issue. The back of the SUV got dead silent, too. I wonder if they think the same thing.

I stay silent. I know he didn't really mean it as a question, it's best if I just keep to myself.

"Christ! No, Emily, no personality disorder, okay. Fuck! Did you ever think maybe you're a little naïve and I'm just looking out for you?"

Tate's cheeks are flushed angrily and he looks like steam could come out of his ears at my little question. That was completely uncalled for. He didn't have to get so heated, it was an honest query.

I feel my blood start to boil, embarrassed by his outburst insinuating that I'm naïve. He has nerve. *How dare he talk down to me in front of our friends!*

"Naïve? Naïve?" Swinging my head back towards him, angrily, "Fuck you, Luka!" I shriek, riled up. "I'm sure I've been through way more shit than you could ever imagine!"

Huffing, I turn back to my window. "Just forget I said anything, okay? Just be broody and drive and I'll keep my naïve thoughts to myself." Crossing my arms angrily I stew in my thoughts. Tate grunts and turns up the radio to a newer song I've never heard before.

Asshole. Dick. Motherfucker. He has no idea. None! He has balls to call me naïve. We just freaking met! No wonder he's single. Wait, is he single? He probably is if he makes comments like that to women.

We head through Knoxville to get to the club area. The lights and traffic make my heartbeat faster with excitement. It feels big to me, but then I came from a small town. We don't have all the people and busyness unless you head to one of the cities.

Everyone is so supportive of the Tennessee Vols. It reminds me of home and all the football fans around Austin with the Longhorns. I can't wait until I have some free time to check out the museums and the farmer's market right by the college.

We end up at an area that has a bunch of shoebox-sized clubs and stop in front of the largest. The building is a dark grey color, and has a large silver sign that says 'OO7' with lights illuminating it.

Wrapped from the front entrance to around the building is a long line of people. Everyone waiting is dressed to the nines, with the majority focused on their phones.

After circling the lot a few times, we eventually park. Tate hops out, rounding the vehicle quickly to open my door for me.

I hesitate only a moment when he reaches for me, and then I grasp his hand to let him help me climb down from the raised SUV. *At least he has some manners.*

Avery happily loops her arm through mine and we practically run to keep up with Cameron and Tate's long-legged pace. Avery hobbles like she may break her ankle in her gorgeous, high shoes. I love her outfit but I would probably kill myself in those shoes.

She leans in, eyes lit up with mischief and starts whispering in my ear. Her nose bumps into me a few times; she's so close it makes me chuckle.

"My God, Emily, I about died when you asked him if he has a personality disorder!" Avery whisper-yells, "Cameron's face was so red from holding his laugh in, he looked like a fat tomato! I thought Tate was going to explode." She flails her arms with mine in tow, "He looked like he wanted to rip someone's head off! You are freaking crazy and the sexual tension between you guys is insane!" She giggles, but I don't like what she's implying. I am so not going there with Tate Masterson!

Rolling my eyes, I grumble, "Ha, sexual tension my ass, he's a jerk face that needs to relax a little. I would not let that man have sex with me, no matter how hot I think he is. He's infuriating!"

She grins big and then squeals, "I knew you thought he was hot!"

"Shhh!" I quickly check to make sure the guys didn't hear her, but they are walking ahead, deep in their own conversation. "That's all you heard out of that?"

Shrugging, she smiles and gestures for me to look forward. We finally make it to the entrance after our trek through the parking lot. Avery and I step up on the curb, me helping her so she doesn't fall over and I glance up at the building again. The sign appears huge and almost magnetizing up close.

I'm guessing that apparently Tate knows the guys up front because he's heading right for them. Maybe we'll get lucky and get to bypass this long line.

There are three tall, largely built men dressed in black, whom I'm assuming are the bodyguards or door guys. One normal-sized guy in the middle is dressed in a sharp black suit with a strong nose and short black scruff on his face. He oozes money and self-confidence. The suit guy turns to Tate and nods at him.

"Luka, moy braat (my brother)."

Whoa! What is that? That sounded so sexy!

"Viktor," Tate rolls out in his deep, raspy voice and nods back.

He doesn't stop, just walks right in. We all shuffle in, close behind Tate. As we get through the door, I hear the men start talking in a language I don't understand. With the music, it's hard for me to really catch any piece of it.

Making our way into OO7, I'm instantly hit with trance-like music. It's like I've entered a different realm or something. The lights are dim and flashing to the beat of the music.

It's busy but not so crowded that you have to bump into every person you walk past. There are beautiful, exotic-looking females dressed in red or black fitted dresses. They must be the servers, because they carry around trays full of different colored martinis and pass them out to whoever asks for one.

Do you have to prepay or something in order to get drinks? This is awesome, but looks so ridiculously expensive. I didn't even get asked for an ID. I'm only twenty; I hope I'm allowed to even be in here right now. No one said anything about specific age requirements.

I feel like I just fell down the rabbit hole in 'Alice in Wonderland' as I take in everything. In the middle of the club is a two story dance floor surrounded by glass walls. It almost appears as if they are in a giant glass elevator.

Well, obviously this is why the club doesn't seem too busy inside. The majority of people are dancing. I glance to Avery and she nods her head upward.

Looking up toward the ceiling, I expect to see ceiling beams or maybe dancers or something. I never expected to see a silver Aston Martin, suspended from grey metal cables above us.

This place is insane! It's like walking onto the set of a James Bond movie. No wonder Avery loves this place so much!

Avery yells, "Let's get a table," trying to make up for the loud, thrumming music. Both of the guys nod at her and I give her a thumbs up.

Tate leads us to the VIP section. Even though the club is posh enough as it is, they still have a section sanctioned off. I walk up a few stairs, lined with rope lighting, to the raised section. The smaller area holds about ten different sized, round booths.

As soon as our butts hit our booth, a server is waiting with a friendly smile on her face. I bet these women make a ton in tips; they are all so gorgeous.

"I want a Cosmo, please!" Avery perks up, eagerly.

"Courvoisier on the rocks," Cameron rumbles.

"We will both have bottled water," Tate orders, gesturing to him and me, before I have a chance to say anything.

"Thanks, but you can have a drink if you want to, Tate," I turn toward him and offer loudly.

"Nah, I don't drink a lot. I like to be aware of my surroundings and stay in control of my body."

Hmmm... Something else we have in common. I'm sure it's for entirely opposite reasons, but at least he's out of dick mode from earlier.

Avery grabs my hand and starts tugging to get me out of the booth. "Come on, Emily, let's go hit the dance floor, I freaking love this song!"

'Cracks' remix by Belle Humble is vibrating off the walls. I love this song too. It's perfect to move to and get lost in.

Avery downs half her drink and jumps up out of the booth, pulling me in tow. The guys stand up with us and I pull back on Avery, peering up at Tate, confused.

"What about our drinks? Shouldn't we finish them first? It's not safe to leave them and come back."

I'm not about to take unnecessary risks just because a couple of guys are with us. I feel a little safer that we are in a group but I have to try and think about stuff safely.

"Don't worry about the drinks, everything will be okay. The server is actually called a Table Assistant." He nods at our lady handling our table. "It's her job to watch our drinks, jackets, purses and anything else we leave behind. She will even walk you to the restroom for safety, in case you feel unwell or need a cool towel or whatever. There is a girl assigned to each table."

I'm impressed; what a great idea for a club to keep people safe! So many women have gotten taken advantage of by date rape drugs or being out alone.

"Wow! That is such an awesome idea!"

I smile at him and we make our way to the dance floors. There are a few and we head straight for the large one in the middle. Avery and Cameron automatically start dancing together.

Well, this is a little awkward. I look to Tate, unsure, to see if he feels the same as me. He meets my eyes wearing this sexy little smirk on his face. His lips kind of go up on one side and he has some hot-ass dimples. *Sweet Jesus, I could seriously lick his dimples.* He's so yummy when he finally starts to relax.

He reaches out and lightly pulls me toward him. Tate leans in closely. He's so warm; it feels like his whole body is wrapped around me. I guess I didn't realize just how big he is compared to me. I always see him and Cameron next to each other so he doesn't appear that big.

He draws me in more and lowers his lips right next to my ear. I can feel his breath flutter against my neck and it's giving me goose bumps. His body molds to mine as we dip and move to 'Cracks.'

The beat is insane on these speakers. Mixing the music with his firm body and warm breath, it turns me on. *Maybe he's not so bad after all.*

"So, little one, why did you decide to go to college here?" Tate's voice has a deep, rich timbre and it makes me want to snuggle even closer to him. If I could crawl into his pocket right now, I think I would.

Shrugging, I go with a basic answer, "I just thought it was a good school. Good place to start my life, you know? What about you?" I don't really want to delve into my personal life with him.

"Pretty much the same for me." He returns my same answer and it makes me a little suspicious.

I take in the servers and all the drinks being handed out so freely.

Turning back to Tate, puzzled, "I don't understand, I keep seeing people take drinks off the server's trays. Did they prepay or something? I don't remember seeing you pay for anything either." I scan the floor again to see if anyone goes to the bar, but they don't.

He shakes his head, "There's a door fee when they come in. A hundred dollars per person if they drink. They can drink as much as they want from the server's trays. It's all good quality liquors, so it's a more than fair price." He gestures to the bar and I glance back at the long, oak bar top, running almost in a large circle.

"If anyone wants certain premium liquors, champagne, et cetera, then they can order it from the bar and pay the bartenders. If they don't drink, then they only pay twenty-five dollars for a glow band." Tate nods towards a young girl dancing next to us with a lit up bracelet. "When they are ready to go, a door guard will remove their glow band so they can leave."

He pulls me back to him as we sway to the beat, "The glow bands have sensors in them, in case someone under twenty-one tries to take them off while in the club, to drink. As you can see though, how everyone is dressed, this place attracts a certain older wealthy clientele with younger women."

I huff a small laugh, this guy could work here if he wanted. His scent surrounds me the entire time we dance, pulling me into craving more of his touch.

"Geez, you must come here a lot, you know everything." Probably where he gets his booty calls he was talking about the other day.

"Eh, I stop in once or twice a month to check out things." He shrugs.

We dance for four more songs until I decide it's time to sit for a few minutes and get a drink. I'm a little out of breath and my feet are hurting already. I wave for Avery to follow but she just shoos me to go on without her.

Avery attends college on a volleyball scholarship, and playing the game keeps her body in great shape. She looks like she's not even a little winded, whereas I probably look like a wet cat at this point.

After a quick break, we head back to dance some more, and Tate pulls me close into him again. It seems more familiar and we start to really get into it.

I rest my hands on his solid chest and I swear I can feel something by his nipples. *Holy shit!* He has barbells in his nipples. That is so freaking hot.

I start to rub over his nipples, being brave for the first time in so long. It's erotic and we are already grinding to the sensual beat. I feel like I'm in a drunken haze, yet I've only had water tonight.

Tate moves his hands down my back until he's closer to my ass. I softly rub over his chest and arms. His arms are flexed tight and I can't stop picturing him holding me, while pushing inside of me.

I close my eyes tightly, breathing deeply to get myself back under control. Tate smells fucking edible, making my mouth water in anticipation each time I feel his breath while he talks. I keep craving to be able to suck on his nipple rings.

My eyes shoot open when all of a sudden he's gone, and I almost fall forward.

He grumbles, "That's enough, I'm done."

Tate starts walking back toward our table and Avery sends me a confused look, questioning what just happened. I shrug, because hell if I know what I did.

She quickly makes her way to me, "What happened, Emily?"

Cameron's already caught up to Tate so we head back to the table behind them.

I shrug, "I have no idea. He just said it was enough and he was done. I know he's probably a little pissed he hasn't gotten to dance with other females by now, but it's not like I'm making him dance with just me. I would be more than happy to go find someone who wants to dance if that would make him happy."

She bursts out laughing, flashing a bright smile, "Are you insane, woman? You can't possibly think that with what he's been doing!"

I scrunch my nose, "What do you mean 'with what he's been doing'?"

"Holy shit, dude, I think you might actually be blind! We need to get you some glasses, like, yesterday. While you guys were dancing, anytime a guy starts to come near you, Tate snaps his fingers and points at the guy." Avery snaps her fingers and makes a circle motion then points with her right finger, demonstrating, "then a bouncer comes, grabs the guy and drags him off." She giggles again, "Trust me, Emily, there were probably five guys trying to come dance with you, but Tate isn't having it."

My vision clouds with anger upon hearing this. I'm so mad right now at his nerve, I could burst. *How dare he?*

"Are you kidding me?"

"Ha! No way, dude, he isn't letting anyone near you." She points at me and shakes her head, thoroughly amused.

"You know what, Avery?" I huff, "Go sit with them. I'm so fucking over that man, and I'm the one who's done! Not him. I'm not dealing with anymore of his attitude tonight. I'm going outside."

Chapter 4

Tate

I had to walk away. I have never wanted to fuck someone so badly in the middle of a dance floor before. When she started rubbing on my nipple rings, I was at my limit.

It took everything I had inside, to keep my hands from just grabbing her ass and pulling her legs around my hips, taking her there in front of everyone.

Then there were all those douche bags thinking they were going to come and take her out of my arms. Yeah right, I would have slit their throats if they touched her perfect body. I know Gavin and Niko, my guards, will teach their ignorant asses a lesson for me.

I peer over at Avery and Emily talking. She is so damn beautiful, like a little blonde angel. I will have her, even if it takes me a little while to make it happen. I've wanted Emily from the moment I set eyes on her but I keep screwing it up. She makes me over-think and not-think, all at the same time when she's around.

Emily storms off quickly, looking slightly pissed. *Great, she has that little attitude again.*

Some steroid induced tool steps in front of her and looks like he's attempting to be charming. I don't think so. This Bratva piece of trash will not talk to my little pet. Did he not just see her dancing with me?

I make my way to them speedily and put my arm around Emily, pulling her in close. She gazes up to me and glares. Jesus, I bet she is fun in bed when she's all wound up like this. She's got a little fire inside of her.

The guy clears his throat, peeved. Leaving Emily's gorgeous face, I glare straight into this Bratva thug's eyes.

"Maya (mine)" I practically snarl in Russian.

"Huh?" He looks at me as if he just realized I'm speaking.

"Апааявляется maya. (She is mine)"

He stares at me confused, taking me in as if he doesn't know exactly who I am to stand up to him, "Mine. As in, she belongs to me, you idiot," I repeat, but in English this time.

He blinks a few times and nods, "I apologize, Shef (Boss)." He looks at his feet as he calls me Boss.

I'm glad he realized his place. I have no time to waste on him, as Emily is silently fuming beside me. At least he knew well enough to call me boss in Russian. I don't need my little pet hearing that.

She huffs, clearing her throat loudly. I know she's about to lay into me. I have to quit pissing her off, if I plan on keeping her someday. She's going to keep me on my toes, that's for sure.

"Mine?" Emily shrieks. "I'm not yours! You are infuriating. Stop being a cock block! If I want to talk to a man and even possibly go home with him, it's not your damn business!" She points, bumping her finger into my chest, as she finishes laying into me. I puff my chest a little, making sure she feels muscle; I know she enjoyed it before.

"I'm finished talking to you tonight, Luka Masterson!" Emily finishes loudly over the music. She throws her hands up, exasperated, and storms out of the club.

Fuck! Why do women always insist on busting out the full name when they get angry? She doesn't need to be outside by herself.

I rush off after Emily. She's almost to the SUV when I catch up to her.

My brother Viktor, and the guards Nikoli, Brent and Ivan are all nosily peering at us. I'm sure we make quite the spectacle. Nikoli's definitely going to give me shit about this, I just know it.

"Beauty, wait, please?" I call after her. Emily's swinging her arms hurriedly to help her walk fast, but my legs are a lot longer so I catch up to her quickly.

I reach out to grab her arm, spinning her around to face me.

Emily

I feel a warm, large hand grasp my wrist, yanking and spinning me around.

I automatically raise my arms to protect myself. If Tate's anything like that *monster*, I know this could hurt. Tightly squeezing my eyes closed, I wait for the hit to come.

He drops my wrist as if it were on fire, "What are you doing, Emily? For Heaven's sake, you can't come out here by yourself! Who would protect you?" Tate grumbles, "And put your arms down! I'm not some goon who will hurt you. I might be a dick sometimes, but give me a little fucking credit. I'm out here to protect you." His expression looks a little wounded but also angry.

Dropping my arms, my own temper flares up, "Ugh! Why are you so stubborn?" I gaze at him curiously. Why can't he get it, that I want to be left alone?

I cross my arms across my body, "I told you I was done talking to you today and I meant it!"

"Please calm down, Krasaaveetsa."

"Krasaaveetsa, huh? I've heard it several times now, what does that even mean? Huh? And what is that language?" I pepper him with questions. Maybe he will just get annoyed and leave me be.

45

"It's Russian, okay? I'm stubborn because I want you. If I want something, I take it. I don't waste time and screw around." He drops his eyes, casually running them over my body.

Stubbornly, he meets my gaze again, "I want you to be mine and I'm willing to lay claim if someone comes sniffing around."

"And Krasaaveetsa?" He says intensely, grabbing both of my wrists and putting them above my head against the cool vehicle.

Tate leans his large body, pressing against me. I can feel his solid muscles molded through his shirt. He's hard in all the right places. It makes me excited and anxious all at once—I've never enjoyed being controlled before.

Tate screams 'dominate' to me and it almost pulls me to him, versus pushing me away as one would think. It's like my body craves someone who can take away all of my worries for once. This is a man who brings out something primal, from deep inside of me.

He leans in so close, our lips are almost touching. His breath coming out in short little pants, washing over my lips. With each warm breath, my pussy clenches. I inhale deeply and can taste the mint from his breath. No matter how hard I seem to fight against wanting to like him, my body calls to his. It's never reacted like this with anyone before, like it's found its match.

In a softer voice he says, "Baby, Krasaaveetsa means 'beauty'." Tate's lips graze mine as he speaks, "I find you so fucking beautiful, you don't even realize." The last words come out as a whisper.

After he says it I nip at his bottom lip a little. That does it. Next thing I know he is kissing me softly, almost testing my lips out. It's like he's memorizing the flavor, the texture, the wetness.

Tate's mouth is cool and fresh and his lips are so soft. I let out a little moan, as his tongue tangles with mine. I can't help it—he has me so wound up.

He pulls back and looks into my eyes, he nudges my nose softly with his, then slams his mouth onto mine. This is it. This is where he owns me.

I pull myself up his body as he kisses me feverishly, wrapping my legs around his waist and threading my hands in his hair. It's just long enough for me to wind my fingers in for a grip and pull it.

He lets out a growl and puts one arm under my ass to hold me up, even closer to him. His other hand has a firm—but not painful—grip on the nape of my neck. Tate lets me know that he is in control of this kiss. I'm just the lucky participant to be receiving a kiss like this. And fuck, do I feel lucky right now, my body burns for his.

We're rudely interrupted by a cheery Avery, "Hey, love birds! We figured the night was probably done when y'all took off outside."

At Avery's mischievous sounding voice, Tate pulls away from me and slowly sets me back on the ground. He gazes at me, eyes lit up full of need with each movement I make. We don't break eye contact the entire time, almost as if we're in our own little bubble and everything else is just static. I don't think either one of us expected that kiss to be so charged.

Thank God Avery interrupted us when she did. We would probably be missing some clothes right now if she hadn't. I know I wanted to try out a one-night stand tonight, but not with Tate. Things could get way too messy with him.

After everything I just went through and having to start over, I wouldn't survive if I let Tate have me and then he decided he was done with me. I know that would happen; he'd get bored and move on. In return, I'd be left broken in a whole new way.

Avery and Cameron hop in the SUV while Tate opens my door for me. He nods at the guys in front of the door and they wave back. Geez, I bet they got an eye full, I had completely forgotten they were even over there.

The ride home is pretty quiet. Tate and I both seem to be lost in our own thoughts. We arrive at my apartment first.

"I'll walk you up?" Tate turns to me.

"No, it's fine; I'll make it in okay. Thank you for dropping me off." I shoot him a small smile and turn to the back, "Bye, Cameron. Avery, babe, I'll text you. Night y'all."

I jump out and close the door before Tate can even undo his seatbelt. I don't have the energy to battle with him about that kiss.

I leisurely make my way up to my tiny apartment, playing the night over in my head. I never would have guessed Tate and I would have that kind of chemistry. The sex—well, the sex—would be insane.

As I get closer to the blue front door, there's a chess piece. It looks like a king that's been laid on its side. There's some writing on it; carved into it lengthways is 'Check mate'. *That's weird.*

Someone must have dropped the piece while walking down the hall. I've never played chess before, but my ex did. I don't know why, but I snatch it up, ignoring the queasy feeling I get with it and chalking it up to coincidence.

It was such a crazy night, full of fun and drama. Kind of makes me miss London's craziness. She was always so much fun to go out with. We would dance the night away until she found her next hot guy.

Glancing at my phone, I scroll through my messages looking for anything from Elliot. I've been patient long enough for him to reply. I'm texting him again tomorrow to check in on everything.

I'm tired and ready for my pajamas. I take my Prozac and attempt to get some sleep because I want to check out the farmer's market in the morning.

Chapter 5

The next two weeks fly by. I'm kept busy with my schoolwork. Being at a new place, I slowly explore the city, taking in everything at my own pace. I don't love it yet, but I'm definitely starting to enjoy it.

I've learned that Knoxville is surrounded by seven lakes: Cherokee, Douglas, Ft. Loudon, Melton Hill, Norris, Watts Bar, and Tellico Lake. I've always enjoyed going swimming. London and I spent many summer days at the lake near Austin. I can't wait until our next long weekend. I'm going to drag Avery out to one of the lakes so we can get a tan and relax.

For now, I'm going to buckle down for the test this week. I never took school as seriously as I do now. I want to know that if my family were alive they would be proud of me. I can't help but wonder what my life would be like, if Momma were still here. That day my life took a huge change, likes to play in my head like a twisted joke, popping up to ruin happy memories.

* * *

Twelve-year-old Emily...

Principal Kegal pops his head in our classroom, peeking around the door opening and everyone is frozen at the sight of him.

He looks over at me with a sad expression, then turns to our teacher, "Hi, Miss Swanson. I need to speak to Emily Harper please. She needs to grab her things to leave for the day also, thanks." He nods giving Miss Swanson another sad look, which is strange. He usually looks at her as if he's seeing the sun for the first time. I think he has a little crush on her.

Principal Kegal must want to see me about our student council project. It's going to be awesome planting all those new trees at the retirement center. Kind of weird I have to grab my things though, maybe Momma or Granddaddy is here or somethin'.

Glancing over at my best friend, London, I stick my tongue out at her. She's so great; after school we are going to hang out and paint our nails with some new polish she got for her birthday. I get to see her cute older brother, Elliot, and his friends too, so it's an added bonus.

I quickly pack up the books in my bag and my new makeup compact my momma had just let me get when I told her London was allowed to have one.

"Hi, Mr. Kegal, how are you today?" I smile and ask as soon as we are in the hall.

Mr. Kegal is always wearing a polo style shirt with one of our town's sports team's logo and khaki pants. I think he even has hats to match, I've seen a few. He looks more like he should be a coach than
the principal of the middle school.

There are two stern looking police officers waiting out in the hallway for us. *Oh no.* I hope Mr. Kegal's not asking questions about someone smoking behind the school again. He's way stricter being principal at the middle school than he used to be in elementary. I think this place stresses him out more. I wish everyone would stop being so mean to him when they get into trouble.

He gives me a kind smile, "I'm good, sweetheart, thanks. Listen, this is Sergeant Rodderick and Detective Saint. They have some very sad news to share with you. I'll stay right here with you as long as you need me to, okay?"

I look over at the officers; Sergeant Rodderick looks a little older than Momma. He has really short, brown hair that's cut like a soldier. Kind of like the guys in the commercials I see on TV. He's tall and skinny, with a bushy, brown mustache.

Detective Saint looks a bit older, closer to my granddaddy's age. He has short black and white hair and warm, friendly brown eyes with lines like he laughs a lot. He's also kind of chubby like he enjoys his coffee and pie a little too much.

"Okay." I gaze curiously at Principal Kegal, "Where's my granddaddy?"

Mr. Kegal exchanges a strange look with the officers, and then turns back to me. *What's going on?*

"We haven't been able to reach him yet. I think he's out on old Mr. Mills' ranch somewhere. An officer went to see if he could find him, so he can come get you after we talk."

Mr. Mills' ranch is huge so I understand. He and Granddaddy are always doing something on that old ranch.

I nod at the principal and turn toward the police officers.

"Hi, what can I help with?" I'm in the student council, so it's my job to help any way I can with school problems.

The younger officer starts, "Well, Miss Harper, I'm afraid we have some terrible news. Your momma is Susan Harper, correct?"

I gasp, surprised, "Oh my God, Momma? Yes, that's her, is she in trouble or something?" I glance between both the officers, "My momma's a real good person, so whatever it is, I'm sure you have the wrong person!"

I'll have to go to the office at lunchtime and ask if I can give Momma a call. I know she'll wanna hear all about this.

The older guy cuts in, softly saying, "No, dear, your momma's not in any trouble. She was in an accident today when she was driving. I'm so sorry to tell you, but your momma didn't survive. She's with the angels now, honey. If we can do anything, we are here to help."

The officers look really sorry to be telling me this and it just makes me angry. They have the wrong person, I'm sure of it. I would feel it in my heart, in my soul if something happened to my momma.

I glare angrily at all three men, "I'll tell you what you can do. You can quit lying about my momma! My momma's just fine. You go see, she's at work, at the diner." I place my hands on my hips, scowling, "You are not very good officers by getting it wrong. You should be ashamed of yourselves, talking about my momma that way! My granddaddy's gonna fix this and show you all that my momma's just fine." I wince because my yelling echoes down the hallway.

They have this all wrong. I need to get back to Miss Swanson's room so I can finish my work. I know I'm gonna have to ask for help on this math assignment now.

Mr. Kegal looks at me as tears shine in his eyes, "No sweetheart, I'm afraid it's true. It really is your momma, and she's gone. She died, and I am so completely sorry this is happening to you." He touches my arm tenderly as he says this.

I stare into his sad blue eyes and know he's telling me the truth. He and Momma went to school together when they were kids and I've known Mr. Kegal since he became principal when I started second grade. I know he wouldn't lie to me like this; he's always been a nice person.

I really don't know what to do. It's like someone just kicked me in my stomach, it feels like someone has a pillow over my face and is sucking all the air from my lungs. I gasp loudly, as my chest tightens. Hot tears stream down my cheeks and the world goes insanely loud with silence. I see people's mouths moving, but I can't hear a word anyone is saying to me.

They are all looking at me worriedly and I drop to the floor. I have my hands sprawled out in front of me on the cold white tiles. I don't know how to survive without my momma. I let out a gut wrenching wail as I feel like my heart is exploding inside.

Mr. Kegal scoops me up in his arms, where I sob loudly. Mr. Kegal is openly crying now, and I hear Miss Swanson come into the hallway. I know the officer tells her what happened because she comes to me and hugs me to her chest.

Everyone, all of my classmates are in the hallway staring at me as Mr. Kegal carries me to the office. I look to London and see Brandon Meeks holding her in the middle of the hallway while she cries. She looks so grief stricken;

it hurts my heart even more. Momma was her other momma, and I know it hurts her heart, too.

***

A tear rolls down my cheek as I remember that awful day. God, I miss my Momma every single day. I have to remind myself I was lucky enough to get her for twelve years of my life. Even though I don't think it's fair she was taken from me, it could have been worse—I could have had her for even less time.

I wipe my cheek, as a text alert sounds from my phone. Fumbling, I dig through my bag until I find it, turning it on to see Tate's name pop up.

T – Kpacota, I miss you. Have lunch with me?

It's been two weeks since we've really talked. We say hi to each other, sit next to each other in class. We even talk about the classwork we have together a little bit, but that's about it. Frankly, that night at the club has me a little scared. I wasn't expecting to have that kind of reaction to him.

I'm not ready for a relationship or to open myself up that much to someone this soon. At the same time though, when I'm around him, I never want to leave. I want him to touch me. When we talk about our school stuff, I find myself wanting to open up to him about everything. We actually have a lot in common and when he's not being bossy or territorial, my wall crumbles a little more.

Have lunch with him or not? I guess I could. Things have seemed to cool off for him around me. I'm still completely taken with him, but I can keep it to myself.

This is good; maybe we will become friends instead of whatever we've been. I don't even know how to categorize us. I am yet to really make any friends

53

with fellow classmates. I have Avery, Tate and Cameron. I know I need to keep to myself, but it's lonely.

I wasn't super popular growing up, but I did have a few regular friends I talked to frequently. Well, up until I started dating *him*, then I was only allowed to talk to London and he *hated* that, too. I wasn't giving up London though; I had already given up everything else. I'm so not going to think of that awful stuff right now.

On to Luka 'Tate' Masterson and hopefully my new real friend.

Me – Sounds good, where and when?

T – Are you free today in 30 min?

Me – I can make that work

T – Good. I'll come get you. See you in 30 ;)

Me – Okay.

I pull on some cute little jean shorts from Rue 21, my hot pink, Cartel Ink shirt that has a picture of Alice in Wonderland. I love it because she's tattooed and pierced in it. It's one of my favorite shirts that I own. I might not have any tattoos, but I still love them.

I think this outfit will work, it's only lunch. I seriously doubt Tate would bring me anywhere fancy like the club to grab a bite to eat. I pair it with my low, black Converse shoes and make my way downstairs to wait for Tate.

I step onto the sidewalk in front of my apartment building and get a weird tingly sensation in my stomach, like someone is watching me. I need to give London a call and make sure *he's* still in jail.

Before I have a chance to have a good look around, a grey sports car pulls up in front of me. The car is a gunmetal grey, the grill is dark like the paint, it has 21-inch rims and the suspension is low enough the tires take up the entire wheel well. The car is full of clean, smooth lines; it's insanely beautiful.

Tate quickly exits and hurries around the car to open my door. "Damn, little pet, you look smokin' today!" I smile at him and then look at the ground. I always feel shy around him.

"Hi. Thanks for picking me up."

He smirks as he looks me up and down with his gorgeous hazel eyes. Tate's in all his glory, hotness incarnate. Relaxed, dark, straight, distressed jeans, plain black T-shirt that hugs his muscles perfectly and black leather Polo boots. He has a little product in his dark brown hair and his eyes sparkle like he's excited.

He's wearing a grin and has his dimples on full display as he notices me checking him out. He shuts the car door for me.

Watching him run around the front of the car to his side, I can see his Russian features. High cheekbones and straight, strong nose; he always walks around with his head up, as if he is in charge of everything.

Tate climbs in and it looks as if this car was made specifically for him, the way the black and red leather seat molds against his shoulders. He fills up the space nicely with his size. If the seats weren't so low, he'd probably be too big.

I run my hand against the smooth leather, "Gosh, Tate, what kind of car is this? I've never seen anything like it! The seats are soft as butter."

I actually sit down toward the ground. It feels as if you could put your feet down and touch it. The inside is all black leather with blood red accents. There is a big screen on the dash and it all looks super high tech.

When he hears my question, he looks at me and it's like looking at a little kid, he's so excited. Oh, Tate definitely likes his cars, and I just gave him an in to talk about them.

"This, Krasaaveetsa, is a Bentley Continental GT Speed. I figure I need something beautiful to drive, because you deserve to be surrounded by as much beauty as I am right now."

I smile brightly, because that is seriously sweet. I know my cheeks are red, I can feel them burning. I buckle my seat belt and look out the window. I have no idea what to say back, I'm a little twitter-pated right now.

Tate turns up the radio. 'Out of the Black' by Royal Blood is playing. I have this on my playlist for when I run at the gym. He smirks, laying down on the gas and I'm pulled back into my seat. This stunning car also has tons of power. I could totally get addicted to driving this thing.

After a short drive, we arrive at a place on the river called Calhoun's. It looks like a giant metal building with a big glowing orange sign that says 'Calhoun's'.

It's close to the UT Campus, and on the way we drove by Neyland Stadium. It feels as if we flew here, I know there is no way he was doing the speed limit. His sexy factor just went up two more notches after that ride.

The sweet hostess greets us and we decide to sit on the deck. It's early enough that it's not too humid. They have an outside deck as well as an enclosed deck with a panoramic view of the Tennessee River. The weather's actually really beautiful today. It's pretty cool because Calhoun's is accessible by boat and has its own dock.

It smells wonderfully of BBQ. I'm a true Texas gal, I love my BBQ.

The deck has its own special menu. I order the BBQ chicken sandwich with a Dr. Pepper and Tate has the Calhoun's Trio with a glass of water. He also orders us the Ale steak skewers as an appetizer. Everything sounds so delicious, I didn't realize how hungry I was until the BBQ smell hit me.

This is the kind of place I know London will love when she visits. I can see her in a bikini top and short-shorts doing shots on the deck. I'm sure she'll have, five different guys offering her boat rides, too. She's always been fun and a party girl. I bet she and Avery would be double trouble together.

Tate cuts in as I'm checking out the awesome deck set up. "Thanks for coming to lunch. I wasn't sure if you'd agree." He gives me his best sexy smirk.

"Oh yeah, no problem, thanks for the invite. I didn't realize how hungry I was until we walked in. I've never even heard of this place, thanks for bringing me."

"The food's good. My brother and I have been here a few times before."

Tate has sunglasses on. It's a bummer they hide his eyes. I think his eyes are my favorite feature on him, or his plump lips, or his nipple rings, or, well, never mind.

"Oh, you have a brother?"

"Yes, my brother is Viktor."

"Is he in school, too?"

"No, he does some business for my father. He was at the club when we went. Viktor was the one outside at the door, dressed like he was going to a meeting instead of a nightclub."

"You mean the thinner guy who called you Luka when we were going inside?"

"Yep, that's Viktor."

"Cool, wait, does he manage OO7? Is that your father's place?" The pieces start to click together about why we were able to just walk in, the free drinks, all of it.

"Eh, you could say he kind of watches the place, but no, OO7 is mine, not my father's." He shrugs, nonchalant. He says it like it's no big deal, like everyone owns a posh nightclub. "Viktor likes to be sort of an accountant and see things get taken care of. He doesn't want to be the one to run the businesses."

I gape as I take in what this means, "Holy shit, Tate! You own a freaking night club?" My eyes probably look like they're going to pop out of my head at this point.

He offers me his grin and the server brings our food. We dig in right away. The aroma makes my stomach growl loudly and Tate chuckles when he hears it.

Our lunch was delicious, and I feel like I need to be rolled out of here. 'Sweet Home Alabama' by Lynyrd Skynyrd starts playing as we sit on the patio and it brings a big, happy smile to my face.

"What is it, beautiful?" Tate happily inquires.

"This song, it makes me so happy." He tilts his head briefly to listen to it, then nods slightly. "My granddaddy taught me how to drive when I was growing up. I'd make him play this song over and over. I was around thirteen years old." His eyebrows raise, and I giggle a little as I remember the pleasant memory. "We have a lot of land so we took his old tan Chevy out to a dirt patch and he let me drive donuts over and over until I learned how to drive a stick shift. I had so much fun that day and Granddaddy called me Donut ever since."

"Пончик (donut), yes, you are very sweet, not so fluffy though, huh?" He murmurs deeply in Russian, making me swoon a little.

His laugh that follows is rich and it vibrates through me. I did it; I made him smile and laugh that laugh. It's like light in a dark room. God, I could fall asleep to his voice at night.

"I'm glad I was with you when you had a happy memory; that look on your face was gorgeous."

His phone begins to ring and he looks down at the caller ID, peeved, "Just a second, Пончик (donut)." He chuckles slightly when he calls me Donut again and it brings another large smile to my face.

"Sure, no problem."

He huffs angrily as he answers his phone, "What? No. I am out. What! Call the Balshoy Shef (big boss), now!" He looks pissed and hangs up without saying anything else.

Whatever the other person said sure did make him mad. I wonder what he said in Russian. It's so sexy when he speaks Russian, like mini ear orgasms.

Tate looks at me and gives me a little smile that seems kind of forced. "Ready, Emily? I have some things I have to take care of."

He gets up from his seat and reaches his hand out for me.

"Yes, of course. I hope everything's okay."

I take his hand without hesitation. I know I need to guard my heart, but he has shown me a kind side to him and it makes me want to open up a little more to him. I can't help but feel closer to him each time I'm around him. He's turned out to be pretty sweet and thoughtful these past few weeks. He listens to me blabber and just a moment ago when I saw that smile; it brought the other feelings to the very top.

Tate swiftly drives me back to my apartment. When we arrive, he gets out also and offers to walk me to my door again but I decline. He seems a little distracted, so I want to let him take care of whatever needs to be done.

He leans over and gives me a soft, sweet kiss on my cheek while we stand on the sidewalk. I scan the parking lot, paranoid, per my usual routine. Everything appears clear, thankfully.

"Have a good day, Krasaaveetsa (beauty). I can't wait until we can do this again." He stares straight into my eyes as he says this. I wish he would just lean in and really kiss me again.

"You too, Tate, and thank you again. I'll see you later." He nods and climbs back into his amazing car. I watch him leave the parking lot, before heading into my building.

I skip up to my apartment because I just had a really great lunch. I'm so distracted with thoughts of Tate Masterson, I don't notice the long stemmed white rose laying in the hallway.

Five days later...

I'm walking out of the Science building with Avery when I notice the back of someone in the distance. *It can't be, no way.* My heart starts beating fast, stomach fluttering with nerves.

This person does have long black hair, tattoos all over and is pretty tall. They turn around and I freak out. I start jumping up and down like a lunatic then take off running.

"Whoa! Emily! Calm down, girl!" I hear Avery call out and start trekking after me. She sounds a little panicked and I probably freaked her out, but she doesn't see who I see.

"Holy fuckballs! That's one hot ass chick!" London hollers loudly across the courtyard when she sees me, then runs toward me, too.

I start laughing loudly, excited. I can't believe she's freaking here, in Tennessee! She surprised me. I absolutely have the best friend in the whole world!

"Not as hot as you!" I bellow back and leap at her.

London is five foot-eight and about 160 pounds so she catches me easily. She's built like a muscular pinup model. Her black hair reaches mid back. She has striking cool blue eyes that are almond shaped and legs that seem to go on for miles. Her legs are insane because she always does lunges and leg presses. She has huge boobs and a small waist, she reminds me of a tattooed Coke bottle.

London always dresses kind of slutty and is a big partier, but she's actually one of the smartest people I know. She had to do a lot of her college courses online to save money, but she's studying to be an engineer. London could probably even be a doctor if she wanted to.

We finally quit hugging, pulling away, but I keep hold of her hand. If anything so I know she's real.

"I can't believe it's actually you, you're really here!" I shake her hand excitedly, "God, I didn't realize how much I missed you until I saw your face right now." I whisper and a tear leaks down my cheek.

I feel so emotional all of a sudden. It's like I've been running a race and my relief just grabbed my baton to make it to the finish line for me. I take a deep breath, loving it that I can really breathe now, with her next to me.

London leans in, grinning happily and gives me another small hug. She's always been great at reading me, so she probably knows I'm a mess inside right now.

"I was missing you and we haven't gotten to talk much, and yeah, I just needed to make sure you were safe and okay." She looks a little uneasy when she says this and I'm instantly on alert.

Elliot didn't say anything in the last text message, though it's been a few weeks now. I think she's not telling me something and it makes me freak out a little inside. Now that I take a closer look, even her clothes are appearing a little frazzled, which is not her style. She's always dressed to impress.

"Of course I'm okay!" I send her a tense smile that she sees right through, "Why, do I have a reason to be worried?" Right as I'm saying this, Avery, Tate and Cameron walk up to us.

I glance to Avery and give her a sheepish grin, "I'm sorry if I scared you, chick, but I caught sight of London and couldn't control my excitement!" I nod toward London. "London, these are my friends: Avery, Cameron and this is Tate. Guys, this is my best friend, London Layla Traverson." I beam at London as I say her full name.

"Oh, bitch! You had to bust out the middle name?" She glares at me briefly, then turns a charming smile on everyone else. "Hi everyone and don't listen to this loser, my name's just London."

I start giggling loudly because this reminds me of third grade when I got all the boys to sing 'Layla' to her. She was so furious she didn't talk to me for two whole days. After those two days I gave in and apologized. She admitted that she couldn't hold out any longer either.

Now after all these years I still enjoy teasing her any chance I get. London is loud and has a bad mouth, but I wouldn't change her for the world. She's been there for me when I needed her my entire life and
has never left my side.

That is until I had to leave hers; but I had to run away from that psycho.

Avery turns to me and smiles mischievously back at me. "Actually this is perfect. Tate and Cameron her, were just asking me if we all wanted to do something tonight. I was saying food, but now that Miss London is here, maybe she'd like to go out tonight?"

Avery turns her playful smile at London and London returns a playful smile of her own.. Oh great, tonight is going to be crazy, I already know.

"Of course, we would love to go out! Do you boys have a hot friend that can come too, so I have a dance partner? If not, I'll have to steal these two ladies to dance with me all night."

Of course she just agrees without asking me. London has dragged me to so much stuff over the years. It's miraculous we didn't end up in jail half the time.

Tate gazes at me while he answers London, "Of course we have someone, tell me your type and we will pick you girls up tonight at 9:30."

Chapter 6

We make it back to my apartment and a few hours later, London has finally woken up from a nap.

I turn to her, "So, don't take this the wrong way. I'm super happy you're here and I love seeing your lovely face, but why exactly are you here?"

I feel bad for asking, but it's driving me crazy. I keep picturing worst-case scenarios in my head over and over. I need a little bit of reassurance that I'm being irrational.

We continued getting dressed for our night out with the boys. Of course London and Avery dressed me up like a hooker after London saw Tate staring at me. It was pretty much cemented in her head to hook me up. They keep telling me the dress is hot, and I look great but I think I appear almost naked in it.

I guess we were supposed to check out some club called 'Tainted' tonight, but Avery won London over with the OO7 theme. Now it's back to OO7 for us. I swear Avery would go to OO7 every time she's off, if we were up for it. That girl loves to dance and have some fun.

I hope it's not another drama-filled night. I don't know if I can handle Tate on an Alpha kick again. I'm not going to hold my breath, knowing London's shenanigans.

London mumbles, "Look, Emily, let's have a little fun tonight. I just got here and want to have a good time with you guys. We can talk about all the serious stuff tomorrow, okay?"

She has looked pretty stressed out since I first saw her at the university. It looks like she could use some more sleep too, which is weird for my friend. At least she got in a short nap today.

I nod and smile; it's fake but I want to reassure her, "Okay, that sounds like a plan, and don't forget we are checking out one of the lakes this weekend. I don't care if both of you are rocking hangovers or not! It'll be even more fun now that you are going with Avery and me."

I'm so happy London and Avery have hit it off and have become fast friends.

She chuckles, "Us hungover? Oh no, girly, I'm in town, you can relax for a night or two or three. It will be perfectly fine to have some drinks and cut loose with all of us around you."

London's shooting me her annoyed look where she scrunches up her eyebrows and has a line down the center of her forehead. Speaking of lines, I know how to distract her from talking me into making bad decisions and getting plowed with them.

"Wow, when you make that face it shows a big line in your forehead. Are you getting wrinkles, London?   It looks like you might be getting too much sun." Avery busts out laughing at me. Damn it, she caught on to my distraction.

"Don't listen to her, London; she's trying to get you off topic." She gives me a big shit-eating grin.

"You suck, Avery! You're fired!"

Avery giggles, "Nope. You already fired me at the coffee shop, so technically you can't fire me anymore!"

I think about lunging at her and tackling her to the ground. I know once I get her there London will at least help me tickle her. Right as I go to make my move, there's a knock on my apartment door.

Avery jumps up really fast and practically runs to the door to answer it. She must be a little excited to see Cameron. *Or not.*

She completely ignores Cameron as he walks in. Avery hurriedly gives the big guy they brought with them an excited hug. I'll have to ask her about that later.

Cam puts on a wide smile, "Ladies, ladies, ladies, are we ready to have some fun?" Cam's voice booms through my tiny apartment.

London eats up the loudness and gravitates toward Cameron as soon as he sees her. They both eye-fuck each other while Avery talks to the new hot, blond guy. Wow, never would have predicted this one.

Tate gives me a soft smile and walks toward me. He leans down and sweetly kisses me on my cheek. My heart melts a little at the touch of his lips.

"Hey, little pet, you look breathtaking. I love this dress on you. I'm going to have to break some guy's knees tonight, huh?"

Break some knees? Who says that? I look at him like he's lost his mind and it makes him chuckle. Yeah, definitely no personality disorder here! *Right.*

"Relax, Krasaaveetsa, I'm only joking. I'd have Nikoli here do it for me." He smirks towards the other guy that came with them.

Nikoli is a beast. He's huge, full of muscles, probably 6'5" and covered in tribal tattoos. He's still really good looking for being so big; he has short blond hair and dark blue eyes. He looks like the ultimate Russian fighter.

Nikoli grins down at me and I look at Tate. I have to admit, a man that big really does frighten me inside. He looks so friendly, but I'm still shaky towards men in general. Not so much with Tate, but everyone else.

Tate squeezes my bicep softly, "Emily, this is Nikoli, he was a bouncer at OO7 when we went last time." He nods toward him and looks back at me, "Nikoli, this is my Krasaaveetsa, Emily." He looks really excited to be introducing me. I think he may have told Nikoli about me already.

"Nice to meet you, Nikoli."

I stick my hand out being courteous and Nikoli grabs me with both of his big, meaty paw-like hands. He brings me in for a hug and I think I squeak.

"Preevyetstvavats Shef dyevooshka (Welcome Bosses lady)." Tate beams a smile after Nikoli speaks.

I glance between both of them, puzzled. "Huh?"

Nikoli looks at me sheepishly and grins so his dimples pop out. Such a cutie.

"I apologize. I speak Russian so much, that sometimes it automatically comes out. I said Welcome..." Tate shakes his head minutely but I still catch it. "Umm, lady," he finishes, nodding.

Hmm, I wonder what he really said. I won't ask Tate right now, but I am curious. Hopefully I can remember some of it to Google later.

Everyone's heading toward the door, so I guess it's that time. I grab my small purse and shuffle out the door behind them. I lock up and follow them outside.

Tate has his large, black Tahoe again, so we can all ride together and have a designated driver. I get little flutters inside, thinking about how thoughtful he really is. He's always looking out for my comfort level and I don't know if he even realizes he does it.

Tate starts to bark orders as soon as we reach the vehicle, "You girls will have to sit on Cam and Nikoli's laps. Emily, you will sit in the front with me." Everyone jumps into action and I just stand there. *Yeah, I don't think so.* I don't take orders from men anymore.

This reminds me, I need to check out the parking lot. I start scanning all the vehicles and my surroundings. There are lights outside but there are too many dark spots for me to see everything.

At least I'm surrounded by three big men. I don't have to completely freak out right now, about being outside in the dark. I still feel like I'm being watched everywhere I go and I have to make myself stop this madness. I'm going to get an ulcer with the worrying all the time.

Turning to Tate, I argue, "Umm, why, Tate, that doesn't make sense. Let Nikoli sit up front, because we will all fit better in the back."

"Come, Krasaaveetsa, get in the front." Tate replies with a stern look and I just roll my eyes at him.

"No, Tate, I'm not jumping because you say so. This doesn't make sense and I know I'm right. You need to give in on this one."

This man is always making me feel like a teenager around him. I mean technically twenty is very young, but he makes me feel fifteen. I'm always angry, turned on, arguing or feeling like I'm falling head over heels for him. I thought this was what happened when you were young, not in college.

He grumbles, "I didn't ask you to jump, I asked you to sit down."

Tate must realize this is going to be a battle because before I can get a response out, he picks me up. Nikoli opens the front door and Tate shoves me in the front seat. Nikoli smiles really big at me and shuts the door quickly.

I'm so shocked it doesn't even register what they just did for a few seconds. I feel my mouth gaping and physically reach up to cover it. The balls on these men are uncanny.

Tate gets in the SUV and gazes at me; I can only stare at him with my mouth open. I cannot believe that just happened. I don't know whether to be pissed off or turned on right now.

Avery sits in the back giggling like it's the greatest thing ever and London's looking at Tate like he hung the moon. Freaks, damn freaks, I'm surrounded by crazies.

The next morning...

"Oh My God, my head! What time is it? What happened last night?"

Is that Avery's scratchy-ass voice I hear pounding into my head? Why is she yelling?

"Dude, shut up! And go back to sleep." That sleepy voice is definitely London's, so she really is here after all.

Avery chokes out, "Fuck, I'm going to be sick!" She runs to the bathroom but trips over me and goes flying onto another body under a comforter. I want to laugh at her because it was hilarious, but my head and stomach hurt too badly.

She mumbles, scrambling to get up, "Oof. Shit! Sorry!" She takes off running again. I hear her slam the bathroom door and we all let out a collective groan.

Tate peeks his head up out of the blanket that Avery just tripped on and looks over at me. He looks absolutely adorable, like a sleepy puppy. Only hot, and male, with bed head, and wow, yep, no shirt on.

He leans up so the blanket falls to his stomach and I can't look away from his gorgeous body. Tattoos cover his pecs and little barbells adorn each nipple. He is ripped, way more so than I had thought from dancing with him. He has a little happy trail of brown hair that leads over his six pack. *He has a freaking six pack! Of course he does.*

Tate slowly leans toward me and kisses my forehead and whispers softly, "Morning, baby." I melt a little inside when he says it so naturally, like it happens daily. I give him a small smile because he just made this horrible hangover a little better by being here when I first woke up.

"Good morning, Tate."

I start to lean up also, but freak when the blanket falls down. I scramble to pull the blanket back over my chest swiftly. Damn it, Tate just got an eye full!

"Holy fuck! Why am I naked?"

Tate gives me his grin and the dimples come out to play. Oh no, here it comes.

"Well, last night all of you ladies decided to sleep naked." Tate chuckles, gesturing to me, "You all decided it would be one less thing you had to worry about in the morning. I tried to get you to keep at least your panties and bra on, but you wouldn't hear of it." I feel my face start to burn and know it's probably red as a cherry.

"I got you to lie down under the blanket, but you made me promise I'd stay right beside you or you would take the blanket off. You said something about being scared and needing me to protect you. I stayed because I swear if either one of these fuckers looked at you, I'd be throwing blows. I told you to relax, that I'll always keep you safe. You kissed me pretty sloppily and told me you like me way too much. Then you snuggled into me and passed right out." He finishes, flashing that adoring stare in my direction.

Good lord, I'm mortified at this moment. There is a reason I don't drink. I tend to binge drink when I do, and then I can't remember anything the next day.

"Oh my gosh! I'm so sorry I put you through that. That's just awful, I'm so embarrassed!"

Cameron starts chuckling and lifts his head up to look over at me. *Oh God, what now?*

"Are you kidding, Emily? Tate was in heaven. You were naked, and you're bangin', by the way. Not only were you showing your boy the goods, but he got to take care of you and boss you around last night. I think you just fulfilled one of his secret fantasies!" Cam starts laughing some more at the face I make; I guess you can call it disgruntled. Yep, I'm disgruntled.

He groans, "Ow. Shit. My head is killing me." Cameron winces and puts the blanket over his head again. Thank God, no more stories out of him!

"Good, that's what you deserve for making Emily embarrassed." Tate is looking over toward where Cam is lying like he wants to strangle him.

"Shh! Please, Boss!" That was Nikoli.

Geez, did everyone stay here last night? I guess so, if Tate is here, considering he was the one who drove everyone. I can't believe I even had enough blankets. Looking around I see there are actually only three

69

blankets out. Guess I'm not the only one who was snuggled up to someone last night. I see the spot is empty next to Nikoli, so that means Avery must have slept beside him.

She comes out of the bathroom sluggishly and looking a little green. Avery has a bright peach towel wrapped tightly around her.

I mutter, "Surprise! I see you discovered you're naked also?!" I don't say it too loudly because my head is pounding but I do say it full of sarcasm. I need to find my Excedrin at this point.

"Huh? Oh, yeah. No biggie, Nikoli is naked, too. We had fun being naked together." She grins elatedly and crawls back under the blanket with Nikoli. Well that answers some of my questions for her.

Groaning, I lean over, "Ugh, this is why I don't drink. I'm never drinking like that again." I scoop up my shirt and lie back down. I know I can get it back on underneath the covers.

London huffs, "Yes, you are. We are going to the lake later and probably that river restaurant place y'all told me about." She perks up a little and I just want to throw something at her. I look around and spot one of my flip flops.

"Oof!" says a deep voice. Shit, that was Cam, not London. I pick up my other flip flop and chuck it a little harder.

"Fuck!" Yep, that's London. Well that just put a smile on my face.

Tate pulls my back in close to his chest and wraps his arms around me tight. I feel his nose and lips close to my neck and his breaths tickle the back of my neck. My nipples get hard from it and I squeeze my legs together to try to relieve some of the ache he has put there. I swear I feel his teeth graze my neck and it turns me on like crazy.

Tate whispers "Sleep, my Krasaaveetsa, I have you."

And I do, I sleep the best that I have in months.

***

I slowly start to wake up and look around the living room. Tate and Nikoli are missing. I see London and Cameron spooning on the couch watching a movie and I hear the shower going. I'm guessing Avery is in the shower since she brought clothes with her to stay the night.

I check out the clock and see it's already noon. Wow. I can't believe the girls are up and moving around already. I was expecting to have to drag them out of the blankets and yell loudly to get them awake.

I rasp, "Mornin', where is everyone?" I ask the room in general.

Cameron pops his head up and looks at me. He's so tall his feet hang over the arm of the couch. I can't believe they can both fit on that couch together, with his size and London's butt. He has the cute lazy look going on. His hair has a bad case of bed head, going every which way like Tate's earlier. His eyes are the color of Hershey's chocolate and he has long, pretty eyelashes. He's always so put together and all preppy looking when I see him. Seeing him relaxed and lounging around actually makes him look so much cuter. He kind of reminds me of a muscular pretty-boy.

Cameron and London look absolutely beautiful together; I bet they would have little babies that would look like models. Ha! That's silly, London and Cameron are both hardcore players, there's no point me even going there.

"Tate and Nikoli left to shower, change, get me some clothes and pick up one of the boats. Avery's feeling better so she's in the shower right now. I think she's trying to be ready before Nikoli gets back. She was rushing around all crazy as soon as he left."

I look at Cameron like he's speaking Chinese. Did he just say one of the boats? Freaking spoiled boys!

"Umm, boat?" I repeat like I don't know how to use my words.

"Yeah, you said you wanted to go to the lake or river, right? Tate's family has a few boats so he went to go get one. He wants you to be pleased, so he was going to pick up a chest of drinks and everything we would need."

He uses his hands to make quote marks and tries to sound like Tate when he talks, "Tate said he wants everyone to be ready to go whenever you want to leave." Cameron huffs then goes back to talking normally, "They should be back anytime; they've been gone for a while."

I just stare at Cam, because...I mean...shit. I really don't know what to even say. Tate is thinking of me yet again. He's even going out of his way to make me happy, just like he did that first night and like last night.

I leisurely trek into the kitchen to get some caffeine. I need to wake up. On the counter there is a white, long stemmed calla lily.

"Hey, who got the flower?" I ask no one in general again. I'm still stuck in zombie mode.

"Oh, Tate brought it in and set it on the counter." London opens her pretty little mouth for the first time. Cameron must be doing something right, to keep that one so quiet. It's like he has her tamed or something right now.

Tate is so sweet. I don't remember him buying me a flower, but then I don't even remember coming home, so yeah.

Avery comes breezing out of the shower looking all brand new. You'd never guess she was blowing chunks this morning. She has on a hot pink bikini top, white jean shorts and white flip flops. She looks adorable. Avery has her hair down and brushed straight, with just a little mascara on her face. She actually looks younger than usual with her makeup missing.

"Geez, sweets, you are rocking some serious abs! Playing volleyball sure does agree with you."

I'm not a fan of abs on chicks; I think it's not really a feminine look. I have always believed women are meant to look a little softer and men are supposed to be hard and full of muscle. She sure can pull it off though; she looks hot.

She grins, "Thanks, Em. I quit the team though."

"What? I thought you were on scholarship?"

"I was but I ended up getting an academic scholarship because of my grades. It's not as good as the other, but I'm able to switch over to Accounting as my major. Now I won't have to train as much either. It was just getting old."

"As long as you're happy, Avery," I reply, giving her a worried look. She doesn't like to really be tied down to anything and I'm concerned about her not completing her degree. It's not really my business though.

I hop in the shower long enough to do a quick upkeep and wash my hair. I have a new red bikini I'm going to try out today.

Tate seems to like it when I'm wearing red, pink or black the most. He's been going out of his way for me, so I'm going to wear a color he likes. Plus, I want his attention on me and with Avery and London's hot bodies, he might get distracted.

I put lots of lotion on since I'm going to be in the sun, some mascara, and lip gloss. That's as good as it's going to get. I hurry, knowing London and Cameron need to get in here, too.

I step out of the bathroom and am instantly assaulted with the delicious smell of cheeseburgers. *Yum.* I feel like I could eat a horse right now and drink about a gallon of water. That smells amazing.

London turns towards me when she hears me open the bathroom door. "There she is! Girl, this guy is out here trying to get us all to hurry up! Please tell your man to calm down, that you're not ready to leave yet either."

She is smiling brightly at me from teasing Tate. When I glance at Tate, he's looking at the ground a little bashful. I just roll my eyes at her. She's never going to stop picking on Tate if he lets her get away with it.

Ignoring her, I ask Tate, "Is that burgers I smell? God, it smells really good!"

"Yes, I stopped and got Freddy's. I figured the greasy food might help everyone feel a little better." He gives me a shy smile.

Oh my, Tate Masterson bashful and shy?! Where did the stubborn alpha go that I'm used to seeing? I really like it that he's showing me this side of him.

I nod, "That sounds wonderful, Tate, thanks for being so thoughtful."

I go up on my tippy toes and give him a quick chaste kiss on the lips. He briefly hugs me to him and kisses my forehead. I get rewarded with his handsome smile afterwards.

London and Cameron shower together. That's an experience alone, with all the noise he has her making in there. That bitch is totally cleaning my shower before she goes back home. It definitely sounds like Cam knows what he's doing in there.

Afterwards, she walks out in a black bikini, full of cheesy smiles.

I just shake my head at her, amused, "Okay can we please go now? Everyone's had plenty of time to get ready." I glance at each of them, "Hey, where's Nikoli?" I ask, scanning the apartment.

"He's checking out all the stuff on the boat. I told him to make sure we had plenty of life jackets, towels, that kind of stuff," Tate responds and gestures toward the window that faces the parking lot.

"Awesome! Thank you so much for getting your boat, Tate, you've made me even more excited than I already was!" I gaze at him gratefully. He keeps stealing little pieces of me that I'm trying not to give away.

I ask the first thing that pops into my head, "Which lake are we going to, anyhow?" I want him to know I appreciate everything he's done and I'm really thrilled about it. I've never had any man be so thoughtful toward me before.

"We, my little pet, are going to Tellico Lake." He grasps my hand, wrapping it in both of his larger palms.

He brings it to his face and kisses the top of it before continuing. "It's about thirty miles southwest from here. There's a retirement community, a private gated, wealthy community and lots of warehouses with loading docks available."

"Oh that sounds cool."

"Yeah, my parents actually have a house on one of the hills, I'll show it to you when we pass by it in the boat. There are also lots of restaurants and a Calhoun's really close that we can eat at when we dock, if you would like. You should have fun."

Tate has definitely put some thought into this and planned an outing that sounds like so much fun. I swear he just made me swoon. I love a man who can take something I enjoy and plan a fun day of it. He actually looks excited to experience it all with me.

Tate looks edible in black board shorts with little white skulls in a line down each leg. He has on a white tank top with a little black Hollister logo on the left side and black leather flip flops. Ultimate beach boy but still looks manly. I can't wait to see that shirt come off again. I hope I get to rub sunscreen all over that yummy body.

I love it that he dresses so differently than my ex. Tate always has a relaxed, rich look to him. He's extremely well groomed and he appears stern, but he can also be friendly when he feels like it.

"You look really good in your boat clothes. I like that I can see your tattoos displayed, they are so sexy!" The sexy slips out and I shut my mouth quickly.

I'm supposed to be moving slow or not at all, but I find us moving a million miles a minute instead. I know I have issues and I'm messed up about some things. Tate makes me forget about any of it when I'm near him. It's like I just exist and everything bad washes itself away.

He growls, pulling me closer, "Sexy, hmm? No, Krasaaveetsa, you look fucking sexy. I would love to kiss your neck all over and untie that top with my teeth. I bet you taste delectable, all that creamy skin, begging to be bitten." He inhales deeply, and then moves himself further away from me. "Let's get going before I push you too far." I gape at what he says. I was not expecting to hear him talk like that at all.

Now that's all I can picture: His teeth undoing my top and then his teeth and tongue on my nipples, sucking, swirling and biting. That sounded so erotic the way he said it and has me turned on.

I squeeze my legs together for a minute and imagine what it would be like to have him there; his hands, his face, his cock. It's been years since anyone has been near my pussy. It's been long enough. I take a deep cleansing breath and reel in my thoughts.

Everyone is finally ready to leave. We snatch up all our beach bags, heading out of the apartment.

We all file out of the apartment building to find Tate has a huge teal boat hooked up to his Tahoe in the parking lot. I get so excited inside when I see it. The boat is stunning.

"Ayy!" Nikoli hollers 'Hey' at us but it comes out sounding kind of like 'A'.

He's standing in the middle of the boat with a straw cowboy hat that has a big blue band around it advertising a brand of vodka. Leave it to the Russian to be advertising vodka.

Nikoli's missing a shirt and has on some neon green and black board shorts. He looks like his body was made specifically to be without clothes on. His chest muscles and abs appear as if they are carved out of stone; they are so perfect and pronounced. He definitely spends many hours in the gym, homing in a perfect body.

"Nice! We are going to have a boat full of hot chicks! Hey, girls! Sun's out, gun's out!" He beams a huge smile at us and flexes his muscular arms.

We all burst out laughing. He chuckles, pleased he made us all smile and laugh. Nikoli has such a great, friendly personality you almost have to like him.

He jumps off the boat and gives me a mini heart attack, he's up so high. He walks straight to Avery, kisses her hard and then picks her up and twirls her in circles while she screams. She might be yelling and complaining, but I know she loves it.

We start our drive to the lake, with me riding up front again. *Go figure.* Tate sure is stubborn. I remember how excited he got when I asked about his car, so I'm going to ask him about his boat this time.

"Your boat is really nice. What kind is it?"

Tate smirks, flashing a small smile at me then turns back to watch as he drives.

"Thanks, babe. It's a Chris Craft Corsair 36 Cruiser. Are you familiar with boats?" I get a tingly feeling all over when he calls me babe. I'm totally falling for him and it's only been a little over a month since I first met him. Is it really possible to fall for someone that fast?

I think back to the boat. The boat is huge enough to fit probably ten people up top. I had to get a tour before we all loaded into the SUV. It has all wood grain detail and a cabin. The cabin has a table that converts to a queen size bed, a small kitchen counter with water faucet and fridge. It even has a bathroom with a shower, sink and toilet. The boat itself is a rich teal color but the inside is all creams and grey leather.

"Nope, we usually would just swim at a little lake with friends at Travis County. Not much boating experience so I'm extra excited today!"

"Where was this? What's Travis County?" He looks intrigued. Shit, I should have kept my mouth shut. I don't want to talk about home.

"Oh, umm, just a place near where I used to live," I answer vaguely and hope he drops it.

"And where exactly did you used to live, Krasaaveetsa? You haven't told me much about where you came from and your friends there. I'm sure you must miss it; I know I miss my home."

It's Tate though, so of course he asks me more questions. After the past month of being together in class and for lunch, I've done a pretty decent job avoiding talking about my life. I've given him bits and pieces about my family, but nothing about the real reason why I'm in Tennessee in the first place. Now though, he is strictly able to concentrate on me and I should give him a little bit, considering how much closer we've become.

I stammer, "I just, umm, lived by a city called Austin, but in a smaller town, in Texas. Same as London and the only other people I really speak to there are London's family. She has a brother who takes care of my granddaddy's land for me." I shrug.

Speaking of, that idiot Elliot, hasn't returned my text messages or my voicemails. I'm talking to London about that ASAP when we get back to the apartment.

"Where is it you're from, Tate? I'm assuming Russia?"

"Yes, I'm from the neighborhood called Andel, Prague, but stayed a lot in Moscow." He smiles fondly, "Your family has land in Texas? I would love to see the state you came from. Would you want to visit? We could make a road trip or I could fly us?"

I feel myself pale at his words. There is absolutely no way I can go back there right now, if ever. I have been having crazy paranoid feelings already and then London showed up. I'm definitely going to find out what's going on today, why she decided to visit, no more 'relax and have fun.' I know she's procrastinating but if that *monster* is out then I have to do everything I can to prepare myself and to hide.

Maybe even take off running again if I have to.

"That's so sweet of you, Tate, but I have no reason to visit, maybe someday though." I close the conversation and try not to think of my past that is always haunting me.

After a short drive, we arrive at the stunning, glistening lake. It's a lot larger than I was expecting and I can't wait to get out on the water. I've heard a lot of these lakes around here are pretty dangerous for swimmers so you have to be careful. This is supposed to be the nicest lake around.

Tate peels his shirt off, reaching with one hand and ripping it over his head. His muscles clench and flex with each movement. He throws his shirt in the SUV before preparing the boat for launching. He looks magnificent with his shirt off; my mouth waters at the striking sight of him.

"Hey, girly, shut your mouth." Avery comes up beside me and starts laughing when she sees my expression, staring at Tate.

"Yeah, no kidding. Thanks for stating the obvious, chickadee!" I chuckle, "I can't help it, that man is unbelievable."

His nipple rings glint in the sunshine and he has amazing hazel eyes that I know are sparkling, hidden behind his shades. Tate's body is completely lickable. He has cuts and dips all over like he has spent serious time on some gym equipment.

He almost looks like he could be a brawler when he's wearing one of his broody expressions. I wonder if he was a troublemaker as a kid. I bet he was a handful with his stubbornness.

He has a light tan going on. Nothing too dark, but it is noticeable especially since Tate is Russian. Nikoli for example is very white; I bet that man burns his tush off today.

I'm going to have to study Tate's tattoos later and find out what they all are. I've had so many chances but I kind of go brain dead when I'm around him. Whatever they are, they are awesome. It looks like some Russian writing on his arm with swirls and shading, some bionic looking gears on his left pec, maybe the Russian flag on his other arm? I don't know. It's all together in sleeves so it's really hard to pick it all apart when I'm not right next to him.

I'm watching him on the boat as he turns around. *Oh My God.* He has a tattoo spanning his whole back; wow that looks like it was painful. It's stunning, like a painting on skin.

"Hey, hot stuff, what's the tatt on your back?" I holler up at him from the dock.

"Huh? Oh, my back? It's Ares, God of War," he says and smiles big enough I see his bright white teeth.

Holy fuck, he's hot. God of War? Yeah, I can see Tate causing a whole bunch of chaos.

***

We spend the day sunbathing, swimming, boating and just being goofy. Afterwards we take London to Calhoun's so she can check out the deck and have some yummy food. There are lots of shots passed around, but none of us get hammered again. I am definitely exhausted from spending the day in the sun. I had so much fun and really hope we get to spend another day like this soon.

Tate was so thoughtful; he kept coming and rubbing sunscreen on me every hour and kept offering me drinks. He even stopped at the marina to run in and buy me a twelve-pack of sodas and M&M's. Tate basically doted on me all day and I feel very cherished by him.

I've never really had that before when dating a man. I met the *monster* when I was fifteen and he was seventeen. I thought he was everything and continued to think that for a few years.

The changes in him started to show after a while though. I don't know if they were changes or if he had been good at hiding from everyone and had been that way his whole life. I like to refer to him as 'The Monster' rather than his name, because that's exactly what he is – a fucking monster.

After such an awesome day and a great dinner we make our way back to my apartment. Avery is staying with London and me for the whole weekend so the three of us unload and grab up all our stuff.

Avery and Nikoli look like they might suck each other's faces off when they say goodbye and London gazes kind of bashfully at Cam. I wonder what that shit's all about. My London never acts like that around a guy; she's always calling the shots and I mean always.

Tate comes to me and pulls me into his arms in a warm, tight embrace. Even after being in the sun and water all day, Tate still smells divine. His face and body have a nice tan going on and his nose looks as if it got kissed by the sun a little too much. We had slowly gravitated toward each other all day and spent a lot more time getting to know each other.

"Good night my mallenkee Krasaaveetsa, I will see you tomorrow?" His lips graze my cheek delicately as he says this. I love hearing him speak Russian, it's a total aphrodisiac.

Nodding, I agree, "Yes, you can see me tomorrow, as long as I can bring the girls. What was that you just said? It sounded so alluring; I love when you speak Russian to me." I peer up into his eyes and our lips align but he's much taller than me, so they don't touch.

"I called you my little beauty: mallenkee Krasaveetsa." I beam at him because he is turning out to be pretty perfect.

"Oh, before I forget again, thank you for the flower this morning, it is beautiful!" I squeeze him to me as I say this.

"You're welcome, little pet. I think someone dropped it in the hall this morning so I thought you might enjoy it." He dips his head toward mine and places his lips on mine before I can respond. Tate takes his time and kisses me slowly, softly and deeply. I feel like I'm tasting him for the first time, like he is showing me a piece of himself. I wrap my hands around his firm waist and pull him closer to me. He has my face cradled in between his hands as he controls our kiss.

When he pulls back, I suck on his bottom lip and make him groan. Tate presses a chaste kiss to my forehead and gives me a little smack on the ass as he starts to walk to his SUV.

"Night, girls, keep an eye on my Krasaaveetsa for me!" he chortles loudly as he walks around the large vehicle.

Tate hops in the driver's side and pulls out of the parking lot. As they start to drive away, Nikoli leans out of his window and wolf whistles at us. I chuckle at his silliness. We all wave and head inside.

Chapter 7

The girls are talking quickly and excitedly about the day when we get to the apartment. I open the door and choke out a loud gasp as it hits me. Blinking frantically, I take in the entire area.

Every surface in the apartment is covered in white rose petals. *The smell.* The smell hits me and I lean over, resting my hands on my thighs as I gag. I knew my life was too good to be true today. The apartment smells strongly of the monsters body spray I used to love him wearing.

I feel a tear burn as it runs down my cheek but I'm unable to speak, it's like I blank out. I glare over at London and see she's gone ashy and has tears streaming down her face. She knows what this is, she knows what this means. London knew. She had to. This means *he* is here. This means he has found me.

I whisper brokenly to London, "You knew."

Avery looks really confused but comes up and hugs me. "What's going on, girl, what's with the flowers and why are you guys so upset?" She looks confused. She may be my friend, but this is no one's business. She needs to go home where it's safe for her.

"It's nothing, Avery." I try to avoid her question, sucking in some of my emotions that are dying to break free and allow me to freak out.

London shrieks, heatedly, "Bullshit! It's not nothing! It's everything! You can't keep dealing with this alone. You can't keep hiding from this. Tell her or I will, people need to know."

I glare at London as she yells this in my face; she knows this is my fucking secret. No one needs to know what I went through, what I continue to go through. He doesn't deserve to be talked about or cried over.

I look at Avery and nod my head. Fine, they want to hear some of the details of how fucked up I let my life get, fine.

"Fuck it, whatever. But don't you dare fucking cry about it. He doesn't deserve the tears; he doesn't even deserve my words." I mumble out, defeated.

I walk to my bedroom and get my pistol. I'll be damned if he does that to me again. I want Tate, so I have to fight this time.

Muttering angrily as I enter the room again, "I'm not telling her everything. I can't deal with talking about it all. I'll tell you a few highlights about the monster, Avery. First off, this is the monster's work, we don't say his name; he doesn't get that privilege."

I look from London's grief-stricken face to Avery's curious but cautious one and begin.

***

Emily

Two years ago...

I still can't get over the fact that I'm pregnant. *I'm going to be a mommy!* I can't wait to tell London all about this.

Maybe this is just the sort of thing that Jeremy needs to start treating me better, like he used to. This could be exactly what we need and it's all because of you, M. I'm going to call you M, because you're my tiny miracle. I promise I'm going to be the best momma ever.

Let's see, Jeremy will be home in about two hours. I'm going to shower and get all freshened up. After I'm done, I'll cook a nice dinner. I hope he didn't get upset at work today. I know the factory stresses him out. Maybe now he will understand that it's good I take all those college courses online. I'll be able to get a job after the baby's born and he will have less stress to deal with.

I prepare one of his favorite chicken dishes and place it into the oven to cook. It should be ready right before he gets home.

I take a deep, anxious breath and promise myself that everything will be fine. Jeremy will stop being so mean to me all of the time. He's even started slapping me a couple times when he says I screw up. Now that I'm pregnant though I know he will stop. It's not good for our little M.

Jeremy will be so happy to have someone else to love him and show him attention. He's obsessive about having all of my focus. I'll call London with the good news after I let Jeremy know.

I stuff my cheap phone into my back jeans pocket, that way it's ready after I get done celebrating the good news. I wonder what Granddaddy will say when I get to tell him. He will probably be excited to have a little one around, as long as I'm happy.

The oven timer dings and I grab my mitts to pull the chicken out of the oven. I place the large casserole dish on our little table I have set up for us and grab the bread. I pour a tall glass of milk for myself and straighten out the silverware for the third time.

I can hear the rumble of Jeremy's truck as he pulls up. I'm actually excited for him to be home. Lately I have been dreading it, but today is a joyful day.

The front door slams open and it makes my heart speed up. I've developed a little bit of anxiety. The doctor calls them mini panic attacks, but that can't be right because I have no real reason to be stressed.

I have flutters in my belly when Jeremy steps inside. Not butterflies, but I almost feel as if I want to puke. It's probably the baby. Oh no, I forgot about the morning sickness. I hope it's after Jeremy goes to work, because he won't like it cutting into his time.

I smile, it may look a little fake but hopefully he will be too distracted with dinner on the table to notice. He looks grouchy and worn out. The factory and stress has been ageing him.

He has grey eyes and long black hair that he tucks behind his ears. Girls in high school thought he was hot but Jeremy's very shy. I was one of the only girls to talk to him regularly, so he asked me to be his girlfriend after a while.

Jeremy has a long, muscular body like a swimmer. He's always dressed in a pair of jeans and plain t-shirt. He has always reminded me more of a musician. He looks like he could be some depressed rock singer on stage.

I look into his eyes and smile for real this time, thinking about M. I'm excited to tell him our news. I know it will cheer him up.

He looks at me surprised, "You cooked Ritz Chicken, boo?"

"Yes, Jeremy, I know it's one of your favorites."

"And it's done when I get home? Maybe you're finally learning, boo, but where's my tea? Gotta put some more effort into it, Emily."

"Right, sorry. I'll get it. I have some great news to share with you."

"Oh yeah? Tell me this great news you have." He grumbles out.

I'm not going to let it dampen my spirits. Today is about M and our future.

"I went to Dr. Anderson's office this morning."

"How did you get there?" he asks as he sits at our ugly little table and begins to cut into his chicken.

"Oh, I took a cab, I was unwell." I give him my most innocent look, hoping he won't get angry.

"Great, Emily. You're wasting more fucking money, just like those bullshit college courses." He shakes his head at me as if he's disappointed and I cringe.

Suddenly he slams his hand down on the table so forcefully the glass holding my milk shatters. Milk spills, flooding the table. *Oh no.* Where's a towel so I can hurry and clean this up? Jeremy hates messes and I need to get it cleaned up as fast as possible.

I leap up quickly to grab a towel. Once I clean up the mess and he starts to chew his food, I sit and try again.

"Dr. Anderson did a test and found out I'm pregnant; I'm about six weeks she thinks." I grin, because this is it, I know he will jump up and hug me.

"What did you just say?" He growls out lowly.

Oh no, he doesn't look too excited. Fuck! This was supposed to go a whole lot better than this.

"Umm, I said I'm pregnant. Isn't that wonderful?" I ask timidly.

Jeremy jumps up suddenly and stuff goes flying off the table when he hits it with his thighs. I leap up and out of the way at the crash and immediately attempt to hide my face with my hands.

He storms toward me swiftly and punches me straight in the face. The impact is so solid and painful, I stumble. Jeremy comes at me again; he hits me so hard, that this time I fall. On my way down I hit my head on the wall next to the kitchen table.

***

Ten minutes later...

I must have blacked out. I wake to Jeremy screaming, "You will not be some filthy, fucking, pregnant teenage slut in this house. You think I'll let everyone talk about me and my knocked up whore of a girlfriend."

He repeatedly kicks me brutally in my stomach. My head is pounding something fierce and I'm in pain like I've never experienced before. My vision is hazy, like I'm stuck in a horrifying nightmare, only I know I won't wake up to happiness.

My body is screaming in pain at me with each blow he deals. It hurts so horribly, I start to puke everywhere and I pee my pants. I can't help it. I sob, as I wrap my hands around my stomach as much as I can.

He starts laughing maniacally, "You think you can protect yourself from me? You stupid bitch, I'll fix your problem."

Jeremy kicks me one last time really, really hard and I gasp. The air is knocked from my lungs and I feel as if I'm suffocating. There's this huge weight on my chest and I think I may pass out again.

The only other time I've felt this feeling is when I lost my mother. That agonizing pain in your chest as a piece of you breaks.

He grits out, disgusted, "Now, you clean yourself up and get rid of that fucking problem you have. Don't ever tell me any dumb shit like that again. I can't believe you made me hit you again. I fucking swear, Emily, get your act together. I'll be back; I can't deal with your shit right now."

Once the door slams I try my best to get my phone out. London can help me. I feel like I'm dying.

Two weeks later...

I spend two weeks in the hospital. I guess I'm 'fortunate' there is no internal bleeding. They have no idea what fortunate means.

Little M is gone. My precious, innocent little baby was stolen from me. He was condemned to his father's wrath and I was unable to save him.

I know this is not the life I want. I know I have to get away and although I'm too broken and sick inside to do anything right now, I will do it. One day he will come home and I will be gone, just like my little M.

Three weeks later...

It's been a total of five weeks now, since I lost my precious baby and discovered the true monster I'm living with. That is what he is, a monster. I hate him and it makes me sick when he touches me. I wish that he would just die. Each day I imagine him getting crushed when he goes to work at the factory. I want him to suffer.

Thankfully the doctors told him to not be intimate with me for a few weeks or I'd have to go back to the hospital. He doesn't like to draw attention so that helped me out some. Jeremy stayed away for three weeks, but after that he said I'd just have to "get over my shit."

Things have slowly gone back to our 'normal.' Jeremy works, comes home to dinner made, he complains, treats me like crap and has slapped me twice this week. He's no longer worried about breaking my nose, since he broke it when he punched me.

Jeremy says he has to keep me on my toes, to teach me how to be a good wife to him someday. I will never be his wife. *I hate him.* This hate inside me grows with each insult, each slap, and each rough fuck he makes me endure.

It's Thursday now, I know I have one day left of him to go to work before he's off for the weekend. I can't handle being home with him for two full days; he will probably end up killing me. I have to do this, I have to get out.

Once Granddaddy finds out what Jeremy's been doing, he will shoot his ass with his favorite twelve gauge shot gun. I can't believe London has kept my secret for this long. She said I have till Saturday to tell Granddaddy then she's doing it. I hope I can get it out and tell him by then. I know she cares about me, but she has no idea how hard it is.

I'm essentially trapped. I know inside that if I leave he will hurt me if he gets ahold of me again. It will hurt me more at this point to stay though, than it would to leave and him come after me.

I can't get ahold of London. I think she's still at work. I have to go now, if I'm going to make it to Granddaddy's before it's time for Jeremy to get off work.

I pull on my black and pink Converse sneakers. I sling my backpack onto my shoulders as I leave my bedroom. Trekking to the living room, I grab up my duffle bag, and then start walking to Granddad's house.

I'm about a mile down the dirt road we live on, when I see it. Jeremy's old blue pick-up truck is flying down the dirt road in front of me. I know he sees me, I hope he just drives past and leaves me alone.

Damn it! He never comes home early. I wonder if he found out somehow. But how? I have only told London about it over the phone, when he was at work. He's never really told me I can't leave; he just implies that I'll be his wife one day.

The truck skids to a stop in front of me and I start to shake. Don't puke, don't puke, please don't puke.

He climbs out, "Where ya' goin', cupcake?" He gazes at the backpack on my back and the duffle bag in my hand.

I chuckle nervously. "Oh, I was just going to visit Granddaddy for a few hours."

I can't look him in the eyes. He knows I'm lying through my teeth right now. I don't know why I do it. Maybe to see how far he will let me go with it or maybe to try to buy myself some time.

"That right?" He replies in a curious tone, raising his eyebrows. "Going for a few hours and taking all your clothes, huh? You know what I think? I think you're trying to leave me, cupcake. However, I don't remember giving you permission to go anywhere."

His fist comes flying at me and hits my left eye. *Fuck! The face again?* The hit makes me stumble back into the side of the truck. He uses my stumble to get closer and hits me in the face again.

Jeremy throws my bags in the back of the truck and picks me up around my waist. He puts me in his truck and slams the door. I don't dare move, because I know it will only make things worse. At this point I still have a chance of London magically knocking on the door at the house.

I'm sobbing hysterically; my face feels like I was just hit with a brick. My head rings as if I have a huge headache, pressing down behind my eyes. I feel like I'm going to puke, but I hold it down. I know he will hurt me more if I get sick in his truck. I feel my face bleeding and it's hot, like it's on fire. I hope Jeremy doesn't hurt me because of the blood making a mess.

He glances at me and snarls, "That's okay, you fucking teenage whore, we will go home and fix this. You think I'll let you go?" He huffs, "You stupid, stupid fucking girl. I will fucking bury your ass in the backyard if I have to, before I let you go." He shakes his head, wagging his pointer finger at me. "I've been too nice, too easy on you. I will teach you though, just wait. You will fucking learn, even if I have to beat it into your fucking piece-of-shit skull." Jeremy rambles the same thing over and over, the entire way home.

He lifts me out of the truck, throws me over his shoulder and starts trudging through the small house to our bedroom. I watch the carpet and wood wall paneling fly by me as we walk down the hallway. I can only see out of my right eye; my left is swollen shut already. I watch the tan carpet and all I can think of is how Jeremy's going to kill me this time.

We enter our room and he tosses me on the bed. Jeremy heads to the dresser, grabbing the rope out of the top drawer. The scratchy, blue rope is left over from when he forcibly ties me up. Sometimes he wants complete control when he fucks me and the ropes stop me from fighting him.

I have the scars on my arms and legs to prove to myself that I'm a fighter. With his menacing expression, I know that this one is really going to hurt. I can't go through this again.

Jeremy starts walking toward me and I shake my head, starting to blubber false promises. I have tears streaming down my face; I know I'm snotty and have blood all over me. I think he cut my forehead when he punched me the second time.

I swallow, clearing my throat, attempting to plead with him, "No, no, no, please, Jeremy, I'll be good, I promise." I swallow down my next sob, "I promise to be good, please don't tie me up, please," I beg.

Jeremy glares down at me like he's disgusted with me, "Don't worry, I'm not going to touch your ugly ass right away, but I'm fucking tying you up, since you seem to think you're free to roam wherever you want to. I bet that kid wasn't even mine!" He shakes the rope in front of my face angrily, "You fucking whore, you were out roaming, weren't you?"

I shake my head rapidly and can feel my lips start to tremble with my anxiety. I choke out, "Never." I know he will really hurt me if he starts thinking this way.

Luckily he only ties one of my hands to the bedpost and leaves the other one free. Jeremy turns around and slams the bedroom door shut as he walks out. Thank God he's cocky and makes this mistake.

Since the last time he put me in the hospital, I have learned to hide phones. I have two cheap prepaid phones hidden, both set on silent. I have one under the bed, tucked into the bedframe and the other phone is taped under the kitchen sink. I figured it would be smart to put one on each side of the house in case of an emergency.

I wiggle my way to reach over the side of the bed. I feel around for a few rushed seconds until I'm able to fight with the tape enough to get the phone out. I power the cell up, breathing deeply to keep myself from expelling my stomach contents everywhere.

I ring London before I even untie my hand, just in case he comes back. I want him to believe everything is the way he left it, if that happens. Thank God London knows this is an emergency number and answers after the first ring.

I whisper the best I can, "London, park where your car's hidden and walk to my bedroom window. He can't see you; I think he's going to kill me."

"I'm almost there, already. Your granddaddy said you never showed up when I stopped by a few minutes ago." That's all she says and she hangs up. When London gets freaked out she doesn't talk very much.

I start working on my bound wrist. The rope cuts into my wrist because Jeremy wrapped it so tightly. I have tears running uncontrollably down my face but I make myself stay quiet. I'm thanking my lucky stars right now he wasn't a boy scout and I'm able to get the rope untied.

As soon as I'm free, I tuck the cell into my back pocket. I shuffle to the window and open it as quietly as possible. I can hear the sound of Jeremy's beloved TV in the living room so it gives me some cover noise. I also have to listen extra carefully because I can't hear him if he walks down the hall.

As soon as the window is open I stick my feet through first to crawl out. The house is an older ranch style with two bedrooms, and one bathroom. The outside has the tan paint peeling off of it everywhere. Our yard has large dirt patches all over because Jeremy refuses to spend the money to water it.

The window to our room is in the back of the house and there's no fence on this side, so I just have to make it to the road. The distance isn't much, but being beaten and hurting, makes it seems like three times farther than it normally is.

Hobbling forward, I start to run on shaky legs, toward the road. I see London ahead in the distance, she's halfway between me and her car. I start to run the fastest I've ever run in my life.

It's hard and I feel so dizzy and nauseous from the hits to my face. I can't hear anything. It feels like a bunch of white noise in my head. I can feel the dirt and tiny rocks under my sneakers as my feet pound the ground as I run. London starts waving her hands like hurry up.

Doesn't she know I'm running as fast as I can? I see London has the driver's side and passenger side doors already open, waiting for us to jump in. I pump my arms at my sides, attempting to gain more speed. My life is in jeopardy and it's time for me to fight back again, even if that means escaping.

All of a sudden the noise hits me like a blast of hot air and it's nothing but screaming. I hear Jeremy behind me. *OH MY GOD, RUN!* I can hear him running so I know he must be close. I focus all of my energy to run as fast as possible.

London's screaming for me to hurry. I make it to her and she grabs my arm and helps pull me to the car. Maybe I was running slower than I thought?

We pull harshly, slamming the doors and London locks them. Jeremy reaches her car right after we get the doors shut. He tries to pull on my door handle but London takes off just in time.

London presses completely down on the gas and peels the tires out in our rush. He slams both hands on the rear of the car and screams. I don't know what he screams and I don't ever want to find out. I've never seen him look so irate before.

I face London, and brokenly mutter, "Take me to Granddaddy's, please."

"Fuck that! Granddaddy's meeting us at the police station. I already called him when I hung up on you. That sick bastard back there is going to jail this time."

"I couldn't agree more with you."

* * *

Now...

I blink, shuddering and it's like coming out of a dream. I hate to go there. I hate to relive those memories. Those were some of the worst days of my life.

I will never forget my little M. My one piece of happiness out of it all and he didn't even make it. I can't imagine going through everything while being pregnant. I have to keep reminding myself that everything happens for a reason, even if it hurts and I don't understand that reason.

I gaze over at Avery and London; they are both weeping quietly and look heartbroken. I wipe my face, attempting to pull myself together and to leave those horrid thoughts in the past, where they belong.

Avery comes to me and hugs me tight, "I'm s-sorry about little M. My God, you poor woman, I had no idea you had been through so much hurt. I always figured you had a story, but I never imagined it would be like that." She looks at me with sadness and compassion. It makes me feel a little better to have opened up to her, keeping secrets is so draining.

London walks over to us, staring at Avery, "It was horrible, Avery. It was completely awful seeing your best friend like that and not being able to make her leave. I love her so much, I always have, and I just want her to be safe and ha-happy."

I hug London as she says this and kiss her cheek. I'm so fortunate to have her. I probably wouldn't be here now if it wasn't for London.

"So what happened after; where has he been?" Avery wipes her face with her hands.

Sighing, I rub my temples, remembering more of it. "The police took pictures and documented my side of everything. I pressed charges against Jeremy and I gave the hospital consent to release my information. The hospital sent over all of my information from when he put me in there and what the doctor had believed happened in his notes. I guess when we left the house and went to the station, Jeremy went to London's house to try to find me." London huffs irritably, shaking her head in exasperation. "Jeremy got into it really bad with London's older brother, Elliot. They got into a big fist fight and then Elliot pressed charges against Jeremy. It still wasn't going to be enough in court, so London called a few nights later and made a false report. She told the cops Jeremy had broken into her parents' house and threatened to kill her, Elliot and me."

I shrug, winding my fingers together, nervously. "I wasn't even there, but Elliot and I lied and told them the same story London had."

"That's really smart, you guys." Avery inserts and we both nod at her.

"When we went to court, the judge ended up being a lady my grandmamma had babysat. Once she realized who I was, she pulled me into her chambers. The judge asked me to tell her everything, so I did. She said that if my grandmamma was alive she would've protected me. I guess my grandmamma had protected the judge from something really bad happening to her. She wouldn't say what it was, but that she owed it to my grandmamma to make sure she returned the favor and protected me." A

95

warm tear trickles down my cheek as I think of how different things could have been if my family were alive at that time.

Sniffling, I continue, "A few days later, the judge ruled. She said Jeremy showed signs of Narcissistic Personality Disorder with signs of detachment, he has stalker like tendencies, anger problems, shows obsessive qualities and may be a danger to himself. He was denied bail. While he was in jail he got into a few fights. He ended up having to do some more jail time. I was expecting two years but it looks like he has gotten out early."

"Holy shit, all that and only two years!" Avery looks amazed and like it's unbelievable.

"Yes, he had never been in trouble with the law before and in order for the cops to really do anything there has to be several 'documented' occurrences where I pressed charges against him. I was the dumb one and only pressed charges against him once. It was really all the fights after, which got him the actual jail time. Welcome to the justice system."

"Geez, that's crazy. So you came to Tennessee to start over? Weren't you scared he would know?"

"Well, London and I had always talked about this being one of the colleges we wanted to go to together. I never could come to school here because Jeremy controlled every part of my life." I gesture to London, "and London couldn't afford it either. My granddaddy passed right around the same time all this stuff happened. I got left with our house, his pickups, and some insurance money. He had also saved all the insurance money from my momma's death, so I got everything. When Jeremy went to jail, London's mom rented me this apartment under her name. London and I applied for a million scholarships and with the insurance money I was able to move here. London's brother, Elliot, lives and takes care of my granddad's old house and land for me. London's actually been living with her parents, taking online classes for engineering and saving any money she makes. She's supposed to move here next semester to finish her degree."

London sends me a small, sad smile and I return it. "I knew he would eventually find me, I just wasn't expecting it to be this fast."

"Look, Emily, you seriously need to tell Tate about this." I shake my head at Avery. *Not happening.*

I've completely stopped crying now and I'm able to start to think clearer. I have to make up a plan before he comes back again. He could be in the building for all I know. I should have listened to my gut on the bad feelings I was periodically getting.

"No, Avery. This is my problem to deal with. I didn't want to tell you in the first place."

"He can help."

"How? By getting hurt? You don't get it. The *monster* is crazy; he will *kill* me. You have no idea how psycho he is. I only gave you little bits and pieces of my story. This is the main reason why I've tried to keep to myself here; I can't handle it if he was to come after any of you."

I shake my head, crestfallen, "I'm just glad I haven't gotten any closer to Tate or it would really break my heart, having to give him up. I refuse to get you involved and possibly get you guys injured. No way. I just need to clean up this mess and file a report. I have to get every little thing documented this time."

I refuse to let him hurt me like that again. I will kill him before he gets that chance. The harassment has to all be plain as day, documented for the cops, although jail time may be worth it in the end if I'm free.

Avery grumbles, arguing stubbornly, "Girl, you are crazy if you think I'm letting you go through this alone. I'll stick to you like glue. I don't want you to be alone with him, and if he appears or tries anything you will at least have a witness to coincide with your story."

Avery's forehead is crinkled like she's thinking too hard, her eyes burning full of fury. Her anger isn't directed toward me, but him. She's definitely hatching a plan.

London nods her head at Avery, agreeing with the purposed strategy, "Exactly. Good idea, Avery. We need to make sure at least one of us, if not both, is with Emily at all times. I'm talking like basically being her shadow." She turns to me, "But, Emily, I think Avery is also right about telling Tate about this. He seems to know some big guys he could call if we ever desired them. I know Tate would drop everything and come running if you needed him, he's shown everyone just how much he cares for you."

These women are so infuriating. I know they want to help, but they could end up getting seriously hurt. I wouldn't put it past Jeremy if he were to even end up killing them if it came down to it. I wouldn't be able to live with myself if something were to happen to any of them.

I know Tate cares for me a lot, he's told me just this past week that he likes me more than he should at this point. I don't want to take advantage of him and use him, just because it will help keep me safe. If anything it will make the monster even angrier to see me with another man.

* * *

I remember when I was a senior in high school and Jeremy saw me talking to one of the baseball players. The guy and I had known each other our whole lives. In fact, we used to even play together as little kids.

The conversation was harmless; we were just talking about the projects we made in Art class. I made a papier-mâché cow and everyone thought it was adorable. Justin, the baseball player, had shown up with metal art and he had drawn a cow on a field. Everyone thought it was fate so we had to hang our projects next to each other. Justin and I thought it was hilarious because we were both country enough to make cows for a project.

Jeremy didn't exactly find it so funny; in fact, it was the opposite. When he discovered what my classmates were saying, he got extremely pissed. Then when he saw Justin talking to me, it was his bursting point.

Jeremy walked up to us, pissed, carrying his binder in front of him. He stepped directly in front of me, blocking me from Justin, glaring crossly at him. At that time, both boys were about the same height and build.

Justin had short dirty blond hair and some cute little freckles on his face. He was normally very friendly with pretty much everyone. I remember him being so surprised when he saw Jeremy pissed.

Jeremy told Justin to "back the fuck up off his chick." He then swung his binder out and clocked Justin right across the face. I thought he and Justin were going to kill each other that day.

The fight got broken up and everyone let it go since the school year was almost finished. Justin didn't want it to affect his baseball playing (he would have been benched) so he just went on like it didn't happen. Jeremy would still gaze at him like he wanted to strangle him each time they passed each other at school, but thankfully nothing else happened.

I thought Jeremy had fought Justin because he cared so much; it made him jealous and showed how much he loved me. Not so. In reality, Jeremy was just an obsessive, controlling psycho. I wish I had realized it back then; maybe I wouldn't have gone through everything else.

* * *

The girls sit with me as I call the police and ask to file a report about what happened. I also learn that I need to get a new restraining order through the state of Tennessee, not just in Texas. I wish they would have told me this a long time ago so I could have already taken care of it.

The officers that came to the apartment were nice and understanding about everything. They each gave me their personal cards in case I need to call or if anything else suspicious shows up outside my door. I let them know about the chess piece and calla lily. I now know they were a sick, twisted, sign from Jeremy. He was basically mocking me and I had no idea.

The officers even gave me the number to a friend of theirs, who would submit the paperwork for me to get a restraining order placed on Jeremy. London and Avery also tried to get one placed but when we called and asked, the lawyer said the judge probably won't be willing to approve it.

I guess since it happened in my apartment, it's not a reason they should fear for their safety, just mine. What a load of shit. Unfortunately, that's how the court system works sometimes.

I set to work at cleaning my once-safe haven, which has now been invaded by the person I hate the most.

Chapter 8

Tate

The next day...

It's fairly early Saturday morning when my phone starts ringing. I check the screen, hoping it's my little Krasaaveetsa calling to wish me a good morning. I haven't stopped thinking of her since I dropped her off.

I'm disappointed and puzzled when I see it's, in fact, Avery calling and not Emily. I didn't imagine Avery would actually ever use my number when we all traded numbers that first night at dinner. I really only wanted Emily's but thought it sounded better if we all traded, plus Cam got Avery's number, too. Not that he cares anymore.

Cameron's hung up on London right now. That probably won't last long, though, it never does with him. Most people think that I'm the player, but in reality, I only date a select few. I might get my dick sucked occasionally, but that doesn't count.

"Avery?" I murmur, I usually just say "what" but it's Emily's friend, so I'll try to be nicer. I swear, if this is about Cam, I'm hanging up. I don't do any kind of drama. I deal with enough shit from Konstantin, my father.

She hurriedly rambles, "Oh thank God you answered, Tate. I wasn't sure if I'd get a hold of you before you guys came over." She starts whispering, sounding rushed and a little anxious.

"Okay, what's going on? Tell me Emily's alright."

Of course Emily is my main concern. I don't know what it is about her, but I can't seem to see her enough. She pulls something beastly out of me when she's near. Emily's tiny, like a little lamb and just as stubborn as one too. I don't tell her that's the reason I call her little pet, though.

God, when she was sleeping next to me naked, it was almost painful to lie next to her. My dick was so fucking hard it could have chipped granite. My balls were floating so full, it's like they were screaming at me to just fill her up.

My dick just wants to own her sweet cunt, while I want to claim her as mine forever. I can't wait until I can finally take her the way I want to. Or when she's so turned on, she begs for me to take her to bed.

I clear those images as Avery starts talking again, "Emily's okay right now. Shit, she's probably going to kill me when she finds out I called you about this." She groans, frustrated, "I told her to tell you what's going on with her ex."

I growl, "Her ex? Who the hell is it and what's happening?"

"He's been leaving stuff in her hall, that calla lily you found? That was from him, I guess he left a chess piece at her door too and had 'Check mate' carved into it. She calls him *Monster*, Tate."

Scoffing loudly, "Monster, huh? Has the fuck done anything else?"

"Yes, last night after you dropped us off, we went into her apartment. It was covered everywhere with white rose petals and smelled strongly of men's cologne. It was so strong it made me gag." She sighs, taking in a deep breath and continuing, "I thought she had gone catatonic. Emily just zoned out like she was the only one in the room and London was bawling."

Avery clears her throat, then speaks lowly again, "At first I thought you had set it up as a surprise and I couldn't understand why everyone was so upset. Then London yelled at her and made Emily tell me what was going on. It's bad, Tate, like really, really bad. Emily needs to let you help her. I told her you would help, I know you care about her a lot, and even London sees it. Anyhow, I know about you and your family. You can easily handle this problem with your connections. I haven't said anything, that's your secret to tell Emily about when you're ready."

"Thank you for not saying anything yet. I prefer it if no one knows about that side of me and my family."

"Trust me; it's not a goal in my life to piss off the Russian Mafia. So, I told Emily that you could help, but she doesn't want to feel like she's using you or for you to get hurt. That girl has such a good heart and doesn't deserve the crap she's had to deal with." Avery speaks so rushed I'm barely able to catch it all and understand everything she says.

I'm not too surprised that Avery figured out my private life since we've gone to my club a few times. I'm glad she hasn't told Emily though. I don't think Emily could handle it to hear I'm a Boss. She thinks Nikoli's my close friend, which he is, but he's also my closest guard.

Especially if she's already dealing with issues from an ex, she's not going to want to handle all the crazy shit I go through on the regular. It's quiet right now, but it never stays quiet for long. It's also very dangerous for her if anyone finds out I care about her, she could be used to get to me.

It makes me feel so good inside she doesn't want to use me and she wants to keep me safe. It tells me she really cares about me, that she plans to keep this from me. However, she needs to confide in me so I can help her. I can take care of this without getting it too involved with the Odessa hearing much about it. I really don't want my father involved or he will be requesting an engagement announced by me; because 'the next Big Boss needs to have a little wife at home.' Yeah, that shit will never fly with Emily. I'm going to wait until we are ready to take that step and not be forced into it.

I refuse to let Emily push me away, though. I have to get her to tell me about this. She can be ornery all she wants; I'm going to take care of her.

"Don't worry, Avery, the Russkaya Mafiya isn't after you. Thank you. You did the right thing by telling me. If anything else happens before Emily tells me about it, I need you to inform me right away. I'll have one of my men tasked to keep an eye out over by Emily's place. Make sure you girls keep the doors and windows locked when you're in the apartment."

I yawn, rubbing my hand over my face and grumbling, "I wish she had an alarm or the building had restricted access to guests. Try to get me as many details on this piece of trash as you can. I need to have descriptions in order for my men to be able to keep an eye out. Does he have a Facebook account or something my tech guy can get his picture from?"

My mind's already spinning a million miles a minute, thinking of everything I need to do in order to get this guy. At least Avery's starting to calm down after confiding in me. My poor Krasaaveetsa, I bet she was a mess and I wasn't there to comfort her. Dammit!

"I don't think so; he's been in jail, and I guess he got out early. Emily pulled out a pistol last night and said she refuses to let him hurt her again. I can't believe she has a freaking gun! I know he has hurt Emily really badly physically as well as emotionally and you know how small Emily is in the first place. She thinks that he's going to kill her this time. In fact, she's pretty sure of it. Plus all these creepy messages point straight to death. He's so fucking weird leaving these cryptic messages in the hallway. I'm really freaked out for her. I don't want anything to happen to Emily."

"Alright," I respond calmly, even though I'm blistering mad inside, "just try to stay with her so she's not alone. I'll pick up Nikoli and I'll head over there with him and Cam. That fuck head won't be touching my girl."

I hang up and feel like my stomach may explode, just the thought of Emily hurt, makes me want to make this trash feel my wrath. I didn't become a Boss by being innocent. I became a Boss by hurting people.

I don't get it how some fuck can harm Emily. She's so sweet and cares about everyone. Hell, I was a total ass to her several times in the past, she gives me her attitude back, but she always forgives me so easily, each time. You would be a fool to hurt someone like that. And to hear he physically hurt her? It makes me want to gut him.

I'll catch that fucker and I'll break his knees first. I'll teach him to not touch my Krasaaveetsa, and then I'll gut him, like the piece of shit, filthy pig he is. I'll do this all on my own with just a few guys.

If I have to, though, I'll have every single member of the Odessa Mafia and Solntsevskaya Bratva looking for him if need be. He won't get far, and then I'll play with him. He's a fucking mouse being hunted; he just doesn't know it yet.

I get dressed quickly, updating the guys what's going on and driving over to her place.

We decide to circle around Emily's apartment building a few times to see if anyone looks suspicious. After a few slow laps around, we don't find anything. However, that would have been too easy with Nikoli right there, to help me bag this filth up.

I wonder how Emily would feel about maybe coming and staying with Cam and me, until I take care of this problem. I'll have to talk to her about it. Cam might be a trust fund kid, but he trains with me. He can hold his own and is a pretty tough fucker. I know he would never let Emily get hurt if I weren't around.

That's another thing to think about, though if Emily does stay with us, she's bound to find out about me. I've been able to brush off some of the mafia responsibility, but not all of it. I try to keep my personal life away from business, but we definitely talk about things that have to do with the business at my house, too.

The guys and I make our way to the apartment and we can hear the girls from outside in the hall. It sounds like they are giggling about something in there. I'm happy to hear a little bit of happiness after the shit they've just dealt with. "...and then he put his tongue..."

I glance at the guys, "That's London; let's go inside before I hear details I don't want to hear!"

I knock on the door loudly. I wouldn't mind listening if it was Emily talking about me, but I'm not wanting to hear about Cam's tongue skills. If it's even Cam she's talking about, who knows.

The door opens with Emily answering it, and they all appear beside her. *Good.* I'm glad to see London and Avery are staying close to Emily.

I push through the group, heading inside, chastising, "Tsk, tsk, tsk, Emily. You should always ask who it is before you answer the door. What if I was some psycho?" I ask this on purpose because I want to catch her reaction.

It works; she sucks in her breath and turns pale when she processes what I say. God, I'm such a dick, but I have my reasons. I gaze at her tenderly, begging her with my eyes and body to open up to me.

Emily only has one couch and a chair since her place is so compact. Nikoli sits next to Avery on the black couch and starts kissing all over her neck. They remind me of two teenagers. I'm glad Niko is getting a little down time though, that guy is always following me around, on alert. I do pay him pretty well to be my guard, but he must get bored sometimes.

London sits on the chair and Cam sits on her lap and squishes her. She yelps, giggling and he finally lets her up. He pulls her to sit on his lap.

Both my boys seem to be a little taken with Emily's friends. I'm glad, but if it doesn't work out, shit could get awkward. They better not fuck up my chances with Emily.

I step closer to her, "What is it, baby, what's wrong? You look upset."

Emily turns, shaking her head a little and walks away.

I follow her into the kitchen. She's trying to look busy, but she's shaking. Emily tries to hide her body's reaction to my questions, but I can definitely tell that she's anxious.

I will protect you little pet. I wish I could just hold her and tell her not to worry, that I will take care of it all, but instead I have to pretend to be ignorant. *Please talk to me, Krasaaveetsa, just let me in.*

"Hey, hey, my Krasaaveetsa, tell me what this is? Why do you look upset? What can I do?" I grab her wrists and pull her into me so I can wrap my arms around her. I didn't mean to scare her that badly, but I need her to open up to me.

I love how her body fits to mine; it's like we're two wires syncing together and creating an explosive charge. Emily fits to my chest as if she belongs there. I hope she sees it also. I know she feels something when we touch, she has to. I have never been so aware of a female in my life; it's like she consumes me.

She mumbles, looking at the floor, "It's nothing, Tate, just a stressful morning. I can deal with it, though."

Do not lie to me or withhold information. It's one of my biggest pet peeves. She will learn though with time that I'm here for her, not against her. Emily runs her hands around my sides until she feels my back. Her hands freeze and she peers at me questioningly.

I know what she feels; it's the tops of my 45 calibers. They aren't too noticeable if you aren't paying attention or looking for them. Emily only found them because she felt them. I always have two strapped on me. They are if I need to handle some business, and I plan to handle this trash if he comes back around. He will learn that I didn't become a Boss by being a pussy and that I take all threats seriously.

Emily gasps, "What on earth is this, Tate? Are you packin'?" She gazes at me with wide, curious eyes and I smirk down at her. I love how short she is, she fits under my chin perfectly.

"Yeah, baby, I had this weird feeling like someone was watching us so I brought a few of my favorite things with me today. Know anything about that?" I hate to lie to her, but I'm not going to sell Avery out for doing the right thing and telling me. Now if only Emily will get that little extra nudge to open up. Maybe if she knows I'm carrying, she will feel safer.

"I don't know, Tate, I'm just surprised you have weapons on you. You don't really strike me as the violent type."

I chuckle lowly. If she only knew.

"No, Emily, I'm not violent to the people I care about, I cherish them and give them my heart." I murmur, bending close to her lips.

I shouldn't have gone there. I know it's too soon, but I couldn't help it. I care about her a lot and she has to know it. Hell, everyone else can see it. I bend my head the remaining distance and kiss her as passionately as I can, sucking on her lips and playing with her tongue. I love how she lets me control our kisses, she doesn't try to overpower my tongue or take control. I wonder if she will let me take control in everything or if she will fight me for it occasionally.

I can't ever get enough of her flavor. Her mouth is always cool and tastes of soda. I wish I could just set her on this counter and savor all the other parts of her also. I could guarantee she tastes sweet all over. I bet I could have her writhing and wet by just using my tongue on her pert, silver dollar size nipples. I can't wait to lick and nibble on her perfect tits.

Emily grabs my hand and starts to pull me down her tiny hallway, to her room. Her voice all raspy, ordering me to follow her, "Tate, let's go to my room okay?" Swallowing, I nod eagerly.

I check out the hall as I follow. I think Nikoli's apartment is even bigger than this place and he never stays there. He's always at my house with Cameron and me.

We arrive at her room and I take in all of the little details. Emily has light blue, sheer curtains, and a blue and grey comforter on the plain bed. No bedroom set, just a plain metal bed frame and a small nightstand, no soft touches throughout. I see we share the same likes in colors for our things. There's no other furniture; it's a small room, but I'm assuming she hangs all her clothes in her closet. It appears like she doesn't even sleep in here.

Being in the bedroom is not helping the thoughts that were just charging through my mind; in fact, it's feeding all my fantasies. All I can imagine is having her hold onto that black metal frame while I take her from behind, occasionally giving her cute little ass a smack. I wonder if Emily would be the type to moan softly or if she would scream out my name.

She clears her throat, "Please come here, Tate." She sits on the edge of her mattress.

I'm getting a damn chubby already; I can't help it, we are in her bedroom and she's on the bed for Christ's sake. My dick is screaming at me to fuck her, over and over until she gives in and realizes she's all mine. As much as I would love to take her here, I won't.

I plan to have her when we don't have any company. I'm going to make her choke out my name repeatedly; full of pleasure, each time I make her come. I'm not small in that department and I know she would be embarrassed if there were people around for our first time, and I want her to enjoy every single minute of it.

I swagger over from the doorway, to the bed and sit next to her. I put one arm around her, turning her body into mine more and cradle Emily's face with my other hand.

"Yes, Krasaaveetsa? I am here. What can I do?"

I peer at her cute little mouth. Her top lip is a little bigger than her bottom lip. I could kiss her lips all day and be a happy man. She has little freckles on her nose and forehead. I place my hand on her cheek; it makes her look even more feminine to see her face cradled in my large hand. Her skin is soft and fair. I love touching her face. When I pull my hands away afterward it always feels as if she makes my skin softer.

Emily mumbles out, worriedly, "I care about you, Tate, more than I probably should. I have so much chaos in my life and I don't want to involve you, but I don't want to let you go yet, either. I'm just not ready to."

I hope I can make it so she never lets me go. I lean in and kiss her. I've always taken control of what I want and she is no different. I try to hold myself back from her all the time just so I don't move too fast for her, but I'm tired of holding back the affectionate kisses and touches. I don't think I can keep myself away anymore. Emily just completely draws me in and makes me want her more and more with each passing day. I find myself thinking about her constantly.

I push her backward, tenderly and thread one of my hands in her soft, shiny, blonde hair. I love how her hair feels in my fingers, like silk. I begin to kiss down her throat. It's such an erotic place on a woman and it never gets enough credit. I nibble slightly on the base of her throat, but I hold myself back still.

I want to bite and suck and mark her as mine. That will come in time; right now I have to show her I will worship her as she deserves. Emily drives me backward, with her palms on my pecs. *Did I do something wrong?*

She flashes me a timid smile, taking her shirt off. That's even better for me.

I draw her bottom lip in between my lips, sucking, playing and she starts to pant. I breathe her in, I can smell her essence. She's turned on and I'm going to make sure she feels good.

That's it, baby, open yourself up to me. Let me inside.

"Bawg, Ya khatyets poshyol Vee так plawkha Krasaaveetsa (God, I want to fuck you so bad, beauty)." I start to murmur in Russian what I want to do to her. Emily thinks it's hot, so I plan to tell her how bad I wish to fuck her. If she only knew how badly that ache really is inside me.

I continue to kiss down her throat until I get to her cleavage. Leaving her bra on, I shove it aside with my lips, that way I can get a taste of those perfect fucking nipples. *God, her tits are so fucking gorgeous.* Emily's not small chested but has just enough to fill my hands comfortably.

She fits like she was made specifically for me. Her body lines up exactly where I want it to against mine. I thrust my cock against her, she feels so fucking good and I want to be deep inside her so bad.

Emily lets out a little moan and that's my cue. It makes my dick so fucking hard and my balls feel over full, so that I leak precum. I run my hand down her abdomen, making my way toward her core. I draw her left, pert nipple into my mouth and bite down lightly. She's pulling my hair harshly, writhing under me, so she must enjoy it.

I run my fingers down through her swollen little pussy lips and feel she's soaked, it makes me wetter myself, to feel her so turned on. She puts her petite hand inside of my pants and grabs my cock, gripping onto it tightly. My insides vibrate with need, I feel like I'm going to erupt all over her fingers.

I yank her yoga pants and purple thong down her thighs and calves, until they're completely free, tossing them across the room. *I've got to taste her glistening sex.* I'm going to eat this delicious cunt so much, I make her squirm and come all over my tongue.

I trail down her tummy, placing sensual kisses as I make my way to her clit. I suck on it and gently nibble on the delectable little morsel. Emily squirms, trying to close her legs but I grab the back of her thighs and hold them wide open to me. She's not going anywhere right now.

She lets go of my cock and grips on to one of my forearms while the other hand yanks the shit out of my hair some more. She can pull it hard, I like it. It makes me want to throw her up against a wall and fuck her roughly. I lick up and down her pussy lips, circling in on her clit.

Emily mewls out breathily, "Oh Tate, yes, like that!"

Her little sounds are turning me on like crazy. I stick one digit then another in her to the hilt.

"Ride my fingers, baby, let me feel those sweet pussy juices."

She's so tight; her little pussy grips onto my fingers, sucking them deep inside her. Emily rotates her hips, moving with my hands, as I pump my fingers in and out of her steadily. *She's getting wetter, so fucking sexy.* I know she's almost ready. I pull my fingers out and use the wetness to rub on her clit.

She's making little gasping sounds, panting, "Tate, oh God, Tate." I can't help but growl as I feel her clenching. If she doesn't come soon, I'm going to fucking explode inside my pants.

I stick my tongue in her core and move it around as I play with her clit. She's so sweet, tastes just like honey and it drives me to want to keep eating more of her. I feel famished. I keep my tongue as deep as possible inside her. When she comes I want it all in my mouth, I'm fucking greedy and want every drop.

Emily calls out, thrusting her hips, I feel her muscles contract several times and she gives me what I want. When she's done, I thoroughly lick around her pussy to make sure I get all of her cream..

Wiping over my face to get the remaining off, I groan in pleasure. I know I probably look like a mess, but fuck! She's so incredible and responsive to me. *Man...the shit I'm going to do to her.*

"You good, baby?" I adjust my cock, pushing it down roughly to get a little relief and grin down at her. She's so fucking cute. Emily's lying sprawled out on the bed, looking like she just ran a marathon.

She beams a smile towards me, "God, Tate that felt beyond amazing!" It makes me chuckle, she says this like she's surprised. Did she not think I would please her? Ahh, just wait, little pet, you will be pleased often.

"I'm glad you enjoyed it. Emily, I will make you feel even better when the time is right."

"What are you talking about, when the time is right? I just need a minute then we can continue. I get to taste your cock now, right?" She looks at me with a hopeful expression and it makes me fall a little more. A woman asking to please me? Yeah, sexy as fuck.

"No, Krasaaveetsa, we are going to discuss what is going on, what's bothering you." She doesn't appear too thrilled about this, but it needs to happen and I won't stop until she gives in.

Sapphire Knight

Chapter 9

Emily

I relent. Tate just devoured my pussy and it pretty much drained the fight out of me.

I eventually break down and confide in him, sharing my secret about my sordid ex, Jeremy. I tell Tate the secret I live with every day, about my baby M. He looks so troubled to hear about my baby. I recognize it then in my heart, that Tate would never hurt me or my child like my ex did.

When I weep, Tate holds me close, comforting me as he murmurs promises that he will always protect me. I know I'm falling for him. It's too fast, and it frightens me. I know it's way too soon for this to happen after all the shit I went through in my last relationship, but I can't help how I feel about him.

"I'm scared, Tate. Jeremy's crazy..." I attempt not to cry again, but my anxiety level is getting too out of control.

"No, Krasaaveetsa, I will take care of him," Tate grumbles, retribution blazing in his eyes, once he's informed about some of the stuff the monster had put me through. *You have no idea, Tate.*

"What-what are you going t-to do to him, Tate?" I stammer, overwhelmed with memories haunting me.

I can't help but wonder about Tate's plan; I don't want him to get injured in any possible way. Jeremy can be very dangerous and there's no telling if he has gotten worse in jail. I glance at Tate, taking stock, he's pretty ripped, but still, I care way too much for him.

115

"I'm going to make sure that piece of trash never touches you, ever again. I told you pet, you are mine. Threats to myself and those I care about, I take very seriously. I do need some information on him though, so I can have my men find him."

His men? What in the hell is he talking about? Despite my confusion, I love the fact that he thinks of me as his.

"Please just leave it, Tate. I don't want you to get hurt. I think Jeremy would end up killing you and I wouldn't be able to live with myself if something were to happen to you." He doesn't realize just how much of a psycho Jeremy really is.

Tate chuckles, shaking his head as if I amuse him. I gaze at him, confused, because this shit is not funny in the least. I'm being serious about his safety. I've lost enough people in my lifetime. "I'm sorry," Tate backtracks when he sees me get annoyed, "Krasaaveetsa, it is not funny, and it's just so cute you worry about me, but don't." I notice his Russian becomes more pronounced when he attempts to placate me or when he's angry about something. It almost purrs out of him when he becomes tender with me, it draws me deeper, making me tumble towards him more with each Russian word.

"Look, Emily, understand that I am worried and want to help you also. Don't take this the wrong way, but there is just a lot you don't really know about me."

I'm glad he's taking this seriously. I know there is a lot I may not know about him. It doesn't matter to me what that is, though. He's accepting me with my freaking drama, so what could he possibly have that I can't handle?

I sigh, "No, I get that, and I love that you want to protect me and hopefully I'll get to learn more stuff about you, soon?"

"Yes, pet, soon. The first thing I'd like is for you to come and stay with Cameron and me just until this is all handled. We have a good-sized place and you will get to meet Muffin. I'll feel better if you always have one of us around to help keep you safe."

Stay with him, in his house? Who the hell is Muffin?

Hesitating, I attempt to imagine what it would be like staying with them. "I don't know, Tate, I feel horrible enough involving you, but to involve Cameron too? And invade his space? That's not very fair of me to ask him, he may like my best friend, but I don't think that's enough of an incentive. And who's Muffin? Please tell me you don't have like a live-in stripper or something." I take a breath and continue, "Also, what about London? Her classes are online and I don't know how long she's staying. I can't just leave her here alone." When I ask about Muffin he starts laughing and his irises sparkle with humor. I'm so glad to see that murderous look gone from his eyes and the happiness return. I grin when he laughs; it always makes me feel as if a coat of warmth blankets me, all over.

"Okay, look, Cam will feel better if you are there, too. We have plenty of room for London also. The place has four bedrooms and three bathrooms; trust me it has plenty of space. Cameron will be happy to have London whenever he wants her. I have a security system and high grade locks installed, plus Niko is always there, too. And Muffin is not a stripper," Tate chortles at this, "he's my dog!" I start to giggle when he tells me it's his dog.

I bet he's a cute little dog. Aww, I love little dogs! Maybe I could. I bet we would have some fun if all of us got to hang out for a few nights, anyhow.

"Sorry, but Muffin? Really, that's the dog's real name? And is Niko, Nikoli?" I love the name Niko! I wonder why Tate doesn't go by Luka? It sounds so Russian and mysterious.

"Yes, his name is Muffin. Wait 'til he hears you laughing at him," he teases. "And yes, it's Nikoli, we call him Niko for short usually. Why don't you get a bag together and we can all go to my place and then grill out?" God, he's so tempting... But I'm still not one hundred percent convinced, maybe like ninety six and a half percent.

Shyly, I inquire, "Are we going to be sleeping in the same bed, if I stay with you?" I don't want to admit it, but I could get used to snuggling up to him at night. I bet he snores and cuddles with his little dog. I chuckle to myself, that's a cute thought. Oh, I wonder if he sleeps naked.

"Krasaaveetsa, you are my girl, staying in my home. Yes, you are in my bed. I won't pressure you about anything physical, but you will be at least sleeping in my bed, next to me."

I can definitely handle that. I love when he does that Alpha-growl thing. Does that mean I can't pressure him? I would not mind hopping on him in the middle of the night.

I smirk at him and nod, "Okay, but I'm not staying for very long. Thank you, Tate. I promise I will keep out of your hair and clean up. I'll be the best guest, I promise."

"I hope you don't stay out of my way, and we have a housekeeper that comes once a week to do the deep cleaning, so you don't have to worry about that either. Just come, stay and relax, concentrate on schoolwork and we will have fun while you're visiting at the house."

I jump up, rushing to pack a bag. I grab enough stuff for five days, along with my toiletries.

"Umm, is there a place for me to lie out and tan with Avery?"

"Yeah, babe, you can lie in the backyard or bed, whatever," he responds, winking at me, cheekily.

I stuff my bikini in my bag, throwing it over my shoulder to leave, "Okay, I'm all set. Let's go tell everyone else what's going on." Tate stands, coming to me, removing the bag from my shoulder and carries it for me. I swiftly make myself presentable, pulling on fresh panties and shorts, then follow him back out to see the others.

I can't forget I need to grab some of my snacks and sodas, that way I don't eat up all of Tate's food. I like junky stuff and judging by his physique, he's more than likely a health food nut. When we get to the living room, we notice everyone crowded around my little table from the kitchen. *Please help yourself and move my furniture around.* I think and roll my eyes to myself.

Clearing my throat, I cut in, "Hey, what are y'all doing in here?"

Nikoli turns, beaming a striking smile and stands up. He has gorgeous, bright white, straight teeth. Niko spreads his arms out widely, and chortles loudly, "Winning man!"

I start to belly laugh, being followed by a few of the others. Man, I love this guy.

He smirks after everyone quiets down, "No, Luka's Krasaaveetsa, I am kidding, this Texan girl is teaching us how to play Texas Hold'em!" he declares proudly, all excited as if it's the coolest thing in the whole world. Poor guy has no idea that London cheats her ass off at this game.

"Ahh! The game of champions! Be careful with London though, she will rob you of every penny. That girl is very sneaky." I shoot her a smug smile. Busted!

"Oh! Shut your face, woman. I do not rob anyone. I win fair and square!"

"Yeah, right! You win because you play with people who have never played before." Her brother taught us that trick when he was a teenager and kept taking all of our quarters.

She huffs, crossing her arms and grinning, "Okay, bitch, get over here and show me how it's done then!"

"Actually, we're going over to Tate's house to grill out and hang over there for a few days. We should take some games though and have the boys play with us."

"I'll play with you, Krasaaveetsa," Tate mumbles quietly, but everyone still hears him anyway.

"Hell yeah, I'll play with all three of you," Cameron says cheekily and Niko nods frantically in agreement. Those shit heads! Tate is going to bust their balls.

Tate scowls, growling, "Cameron." I knew he'd get pissed. Tate seems to be a pretty territorial man.

Cameron just shrugs good naturedly and then bellows excitedly, "Wahoo! No offense, Emily, your pad is nice and all, but I miss my bed." Cameron jumps up in a hurry, putting all the stuff they had out, away. I guess he's excited to go home. Or he's probably just excited to get London all alone with an actual bed and some privacy.

Avery collects her few belongings and London walks around the living room, compiling enough stuff to last her for a few days. London may as well bring all her luggage since she always needs so much stuff. Her suitcases are dark purple with leopard print. Even the items holding her clothes have to be stylish like her.

We all step into the hall as a group and everyone suddenly halts, going silent. *What's going on?*

I shuffle into the hall, passing everyone and see there's something written on the wall. It's in huge, dark, crimson letters about three feet tall. Oh My God. Fuck! It reads-

'THE WHORE IS MINE'

My faces heats, I'm so fucking irate inside right now. *How dare he!* How dare Jeremy do this to me in front of so many people, in front of my friends, the people I care about now? I swear I fucking hate him so much.

I peer over at Tate, I know my face is red and it feels as if it's on fire. Emotions and anxiety well up choking me inside, it's too much. It's all just way too much, I can't deal with this. I wish that *monster* would just fucking leave me alone already! I begin to sob and it's Tate's breaking point.

Before I even register what he's doing, he nods angrily to Cam. Cam stands beside me, then Tate and Niko take off outside. Tate's practically running, he's so livid, I think he's going to rip off someone's head.

I quietly slip past Cam and take off running outside, behind him. I watch them go out of the apartment building's entry doors. I'm so close behind them, but Tate doesn't recognize it.

Flinging my arms in front of me, I hit the glass doors hard, bursting out of the main doors. I make it just in time to see Tate lose it.

He bellows in an angry, gut wrenching voice, "She's fucking mine, motherfucker! Come out and face me!" He reaches behind him, pulling out one of his .45's from his back holster and shoots three times toward the sky.

I drop to the hard ground, rocks scraping roughly on my palms as I land on my tummy and cover my head as soon as the shots begin to fire. I slam my eyes closed and grit my teeth harshly, attempting not to call out to him, scared.

Tate yells out loudly, "Do you have any idea who you are fucking with? I'm the Russkaya Mafiya's Balshoy Shef (Big Boss)! I will gut you!"

I have never witnessed Tate so torn up or out of control. He always appears calm, collected and in control of every situation. I open my eyes, glancing at him now and he looks almost helpless like he doesn't know what to do to fix things right now.

Tate looks every bit his young age of twenty-two right now and lost. My heart hurts, seeing him like this. He is dealing with this massive mess, all for me.

Suddenly he turns to Niko and snarls, "Fucking find him and bring him to me. I want him alive, he's mine to hurt. He was just here Nikoli while we were inside. Fucking find him!" Tate's voice gets louder as he clenches his free fist, "I'll make that piece of trash bleed. I will get everyone in the fucking Mafiya after him if I have to!"

Tate glances back behind him and does a double take, "Shit, my little lamb, come over here." He holds his hand out to me, "I am very sorry you are witnessing me so upset. I will take care of this issue and you will be safe, I promise." He rasps, his accent coming out really heavily.

Cameron, London and Avery have all come out of the building; they stand behind me and each one remains silent. I think I can hear London crying again. I'm so sick of all the crying, of being scared, of running. For once in my life I have friends who are standing up and helping me. It is no longer my secret, but something all of us are going to get through. I don't know what I would do right now if it weren't for them, just keeping me sane and working to keep me safe. I may not know them as well as I know London, but this group of people have become very important to me and I will cherish them forever.

Tate picks up my bag and holds tightly onto my hand, he then leads me to the passenger side of his lifted Tahoe. His cheeks are still flushed with anger, as he breathes deeply. He keeps scanning the parking lot on alert, as do I.

He opens my door, bending down and lovingly kisses my forehead. Tate then helps me climb inside and shuts my door for me. He sends me a look that I have no clue on how to read, he's so serious, but it's not really a cross look toward me. *I hope he's okay.* Walking around the back, he opens the hatch and loads my stuff in. Tate politely waits for everyone else's bags to get loaded and then climbs in the driver's side.

Tate turns to me and grasps onto one of my hands as he says, "Everything will be okay, Emily. Will you please trust me?" Can I trust him? Yes, I think I can. Do I already trust him? It's strange, but I actually do.

"Yes, Tate, with my life," I murmur. I give him a small smile and squeeze his hand in reassurance. He returns my smile, nods a little, and then drives us all to his and Cam's house.

When we arrive, my mouth has to be gaping. I know London and Avery, who are sitting in the back, probably have the same expression as I do. I was expecting Tate's house to be nice, but this is absolutely beautiful!

He wasn't kidding about having enough room; this place is huge. First off, it's not some college house like I was expecting to see. No, it's a freaking gated, wealthy community. I guess I should have expected it though with the type of cars he and Cam drive. I never see Niko drive, but I'm guessing the dark blue, brand new Chevrolet Silverado parked out front is his. Unless Tate picked him up from his apartment, but I remember he said Niko is always at his house. The house is made of stone and there is a four-car garage attached to the house. Tate does love his cars, so this is not very surprising.

Tate parks in the driveway, closest to the front door and when we get out of the vehicle, I hear barking. There is a large privacy fence, running the length of the house; it looks like his yard is huge. I can't see the dog, but I can hear him, and he definitely doesn't sound like a 'little' Muffin. No, this dog sounds big and very excited. Muffin must know what his dad's truck sounds like.

Tate interrupts the barking, "Come on, ladies, let's get you all settled in and then we can take you on a tour. Last but not least, you all can meet Muffin. Avery, you are going to stay here too, right? Niko practically lives here." Tate glances at Avery as we all walk inside and I see Niko nod at her. She looks a little unsure so I try to help out Nikoli.

"Please, Avery? It would make me feel better to know that you and London are here with me and safe. Plus, we will have so much fun being here all together." I smile big and give her my version of puppy dog eyes.

"Okay, if you guys really don't mind, then I'll stay a few nights. I need to wash my clothes though or else go by my place."

Cam speaks up and smirks at her. "Of course we don't mind! The house is too quiet. It'll be really nice having people around making some noise. The poor dog is probably lonely, too. We have a washer you can use, just as long as you wash my clothes while you're at it."

"Yeah right, Cam! I'm not washing your undies, London can do it!" Avery snickers at them.

"I don't mind, Cam, I can wash them for you," London says quietly and looks at him sweetly.

"Oh my God! Are you serious? Where did my BFF go? London, where did you go?" I start looking around all crazy and calling her name loudly. She shoves me while laughing then sticks her tongue out at me.

The inside of their house is really nice. There is no way they decorated this place by themselves. It actually looks like a home you see in a magazine and not a bachelor pad. The couches are extra big, with really fluffy pillows and throws that all coordinate together laid on the back of each couch. The living room's large enough that they have three couches and two big recliners. The walls are this cool white color with a hint of blue in it and the floors through the whole house are a rich, dark brown wood. The kitchen is a cook's playground. Beautiful granite counters spread throughout and stainless steel appliances compliment the colors.

I gaze around at the brown wood cabinets, the cool tiled floor and can't help but imagine cooking in here. The bedrooms are spacious with huge walk in closets. I don't have enough clothes to even fill up half of one of their closets. The bathroom in Tate's room has big, plush towels and a beautiful claw foot tub. I really hope I get to try it out. Out of the entire house, the kitchen is my absolute favorite.

"What are you doing, baby?" Tate asks when he walks into the kitchen. He stands beside me and pulls me into his arms.

Tate looks so handsome right now. He's relaxed, being home and now changed into comfy clothes. He has on a pair of thin, grey sweatpants and a white, fitted tank top. His shoulders look like they bulge out of the shirt and his colored arms stand out beautifully. He looks hot and buff and I really just want to jump him right now.

"Not much, just daydreaming about cooking in this beautiful kitchen." I grin and lift up on my tippy toes, to press a chaste kiss to his sexy, stubble-covered chin.

I wrap my arms around his firm waist and rest my hands right above his plump ass. His butt looks like it's perfect to bite, just firm enough to bounce a quarter off of.

"Ahh, you like to cook?" I nod, kissing his chin again.

"Well then, Krasaaveetsa, you must cook in it while you are here. I would love to have you cook for me, it would be an honor."

"Okay, I would love to."

"Now, let's go outside so I can start the grill. You can check out the pool and meet Muffin. I'm sure he's tired of waiting patiently outside, even if the weather's been really nice. He's probably eager to come in and check everyone out." Tate tugs on my hand and starts walking toward the back door.

"Oh, my gawd! You have a pool too? Geez, Tate, you are going to turn me into a spoiled brat!" I get so excited, I start to giggle. I love swimming in pools, rather than dirty old lake water.

"Good, Emily, you deserve to be spoiled and I plan to make you very happy."

I swoon; I swear this man is perfect.

We make our way outside and I love it. Tate has numerous garden beds that line the whole yard around the fence. The back porch patio is covered and is adorned with the same stone that's on the house.

Tate has one of those outdoor, covered, man kitchens that have a TV hanging in eyesight, a built-in, stainless grill, and mini fridge combo, with the bar completely covered in stone.

There's a big glass table on the patio that seats eight; off to the side are a few outdoor couches and chairs with fluffy, bright teal cushions. The pool is a large square, with sparkling dark sapphire colored water. It has a built in waterfall, Jacuzzi, slide, fake rocks and plants all on the side. Around the pool are a few small tables with chairs and about ten lawn chairs you can lie on. It's absolutely perfect. Tate lives in my dream home and I actually get to stay here for a few nights.

I make my way over to Tate and suddenly this huge dog comes running at us. He looks like he probably comes up to my waist.

"Holy shit, Tate! I thought you had a little dog named Muffin, not a huge Cujo!" Okay, I admit I am scared of the dog. He's huge and full of energy. Tate chuckles at my remark and at my alarmed expression.

"This is Muffin. He's a full size Doberman Pinscher. You don't have to be scared or intimidated. Did you know Dobermans are the only dogs that were bred specifically for safety? His sole purpose in his breeding is to protect his master and his master's family. They are also one of the top three smartest dogs. He's not a Cujo. He will see how much I care about you and he will love you. Come here, baby, and meet him."

I approach them both leisurely, with my hand out. I was taught by Granddaddy that it's best to approach bigger dogs slowly, showing them respect and consistency. When I get close, Tate pulls me against his body while Muffin sits still, watching how I treat Tate.

"Muffin, come here boy, be easy, this is Emily." Tate kisses my cheek a few times after he says this. It must work because Muffin watches his master then proceeds to smell my hand. I must pass a test because he comes and leans his body against my legs and lets me pet him.

Muffin is very large, with black and tan fur, his ears and tail are cropped and has on a neon orange collar that looks like it has something reflective on the stitching. His fur is really soft and he seems happy. He lets his tongue hang out and his little stub of a tail wags like crazy.

I coo as I scratch behind one of his ears, "Hi, Muffin, that's a good boy, it's nice to meet you." I look up to see Tate watching me with a bemused expression. "Hey, Tate, his collar's really cool, what's on the stitching? Is that a reflective?"

"Yes, Muffin usually goes on runs with me in the morning, so he has a reflective collar in case it's still dark out. I don't ever go alone and the guys like to sleep, so he's my road dog. He loves going to the lake and in the boat also. It drives my mother crazy, all the wet fur, so I usually do it on purpose."

I laugh at him; leave it to Tate to antagonize his poor mom with the dog. Muffin doesn't seem so bad; in fact, the opposite. He's really friendly and paws at me every time I quit petting him.

"That's really cool, Tate. He's a sweet boy, and I can tell you love him a lot. Would you mind if I run with you in the mornings? I usually use the treadmill in the community center at my apartment. It's so peaceful here, Tate, everything. I love it and I'm excited to stay here for a few days, thank you."

"Yeah, you can definitely go with me. Muffin has to come too, though. Also, you are very welcome; I'm excited you are here." He kisses me long and deep, it makes me melt into his firm body.

While we kiss, Muffin wiggles in between us and just stands there. I pull away from Tate and glance at the dog, he's just happy as can be. What started as an awful, stressful day has turned out to be wonderful.

Later that evening, we grill a small feast, including steaks, chicken breasts, baby potatoes, corn and pineapple slices. We all sit outside on the patio, sipping sweet tea mixed with vodka and enjoy the beautiful Tennessee night. The season's changing, so evenings and mornings are perfect times to enjoy being outside right now.

We all talk and make plans to have crab legs for dinner tomorrow as a group again. I can't wait; I am so excited to cook with Tate. Surprisingly, Muffin lies on the outdoor couch and doesn't beg from anyone during dinner. I remember the Golden Retriever Granddaddy had. She was named Goldie and when I was little, she always begged for anything she could get.

London, Avery and I clean up afterwards and make our way into the living room to watch a movie. Muffin snuggles up to me so he's on one side and Tate's on the other. Not only is Tate stealing my heart but so is this giant, sweet Dobie. I'm so glad we have a four-day weekend. I can't imagine a better way to spend it, than with people I care the most about.

* * *

I'm roused out of my sleep by Tate picking me up and carrying me bridal style to his bedroom, "Shhh, Krasaaveetsa, you fell asleep during the movie. I'm taking you to bed, so go back to sleep, baby."

I lean my head against Tate's chest and relish in the feel of his strong arms wrapped around me. He carefully sets me down on the edge of the bed, and then strips to his tight, black Abercrombie boxer briefs. Tate pulls my shorts and shirt off. At this point I'm game for whatever he wants to do. He surprises me by replacing the shirt I had on with the tank top he just took off. It's still warm from him and surrounds me in his delicious scent.

He turns the fluffy comforter back and adjusts the pillows for us, pushing them close together in the middle of the ginormous bed.

He rasps, rubbing his rippled abdomen, "There, baby, crawl under the blanket, to the middle of the bed." I comply, doing what he says. I'm too tired to ask him why.

Tate slides in behind me and tucks the covers all around us, to keep the chill from the air conditioner away. They keep their house really cold, so I snuggle back into him. He puts one arm under my pillow and the other, he wraps around my stomach, holding me tightly.

We lace our fingers together and poof, I fall asleep almost instantly. He's warm, soft and makes me feel safe. I know at this point my heart is gone...

Chapter 10

Tate

One week later...

I scowl into the phone, "What do you mean, you haven't found him yet? I don't care if he's fucking disappeared into thin air, I want him found! Do I have to get all of the Russkaya Odessa Mafiya involved to find one fucking person? Do not make me tell Gizya you have failed at this simple task." I hang up on the idiot who's been searching for Jeremy, Emily's ex.

I don't understand how they haven't found him yet. A week should be plenty of time to have already brought him to me. Hopefully, dropping my father's name will motivate the tracker to find the scummy fucker and if not I will call my brother, Viktor, to deal with the incompetent fuck.

My father is Konstantin 'Gizya' Ginzburg. Otherwise known as Balshoy Shef, or The Big Boss to Americans. He is in charge of the Odessa Mafiya which incorporates around five thousand members in America. I'm next in line to take the throne here and I've been avoiding it like the plague. It was really given to my older brother, but he wanted no part in it.

My uncle, Victor Averin, who my brother Viktor is named after, is second-in-command for the Solntsevskaya Bratva. My grandfather was the great 'Vory Vzakone'; real name, Vyacheslav Ivankov. He was impervious for his Mafiya-ish, gruesome ways and illegal dealings for many years. So, it's imperative I grow into a strong Shef, with all of my family heading up the Russkaya Mafiya and Bratva at some time.

Here, I'm Luka Tate Masterson to everyone. To my family however, I'm Luka Tatkiv 'Knees' Ginzburg. I enjoy breaking people's knees when they piss me off, call it my fetish. My family found it suitable for that to be my Boss name.

My brother, Viktor, has made it his life's mission to not be a Boss. My family finally accepted him when he became the family accountant and helps find disposal for any bodies we need dumped. My family hails from Mother Russia and The Odessa is mostly from around Moscow.

If we were in Russia right now, bodies would be dropping like flies. Here in America, it's a little trickier to stay out of the law enforcements sights. I know my father wants me to be corrupt and sinister with my position, but it's just not who I am. In this situation, however, I will have no problem dealing out torture and pain to this pathetic ant.

I was really hoping one of my men would find this sick fuck, but I may need to call a few of my uncle's crazy Bratva goons to see if they have any luck.

I need my guys concentrating on keeping the Italians and Chinese out of my clubs. I will do business with them, but not at my clubs. Many innocent people could get killed if something went down there.

I have to keep Emily a secret also, just so no one attempts to hurt her, because of me. She's my priority over everything—school, clubs, friends, family or even the Mafiya. Her safety and well-being is priority number one.

Taking a deep breath, I trudge back into the house, to check on my sweet Emily. She's been here a week and I love every second of it. I have come to the decision that I never want her to leave. I have also decided that I have been patient long enough. For a man who has never had to wait to fuck a woman, I think I've done very well.

I find my Krasaaveetsa in her kitchen. I gave it to her. She thinks I'm joking when I tell her that, but I'm not. Hell, she can have the whole house if she wants it. I'll even build her a bigger house if that's what makes her happy. I know no amount of money or things will matter to her though and it only makes me care for her even more.

I feel like I live to see my Emily smile; it's become sort of a goal for me every day. I try to see how many times I can put a bright light on her face; she deserves a piece of happiness after a life so sad. I don't think she knows it, but she takes my breath away each time she smiles like that.

Emily

I'm busy looking at my magazine on the counter, when Tate walks into the kitchen. He has black leather bar stools that have fast become one of my favorite seats in the house. I love how the breakfast bar is located in the middle of the kitchen, so I can watch him as he prepares and cooks different meals for us. I never knew a man in the kitchen could be so sexy, but when he cooks yummy food and is shirtless, well, it takes the cake.

I feel strong arms wrap firmly around me and I relish the feeling. I snuggle back into him, closing my eyes for a brief moment, resting my head on his shoulder. "Hey, handsome, you done with your business call?"

"I sure am, Krasaaveetsa," he croons in my ear and starts to kiss on my neck. *God that feels amazing.* I learned at my apartment that Tate is very, very talented with that mouth.

I turn in my seat so I'm facing him. I want to kiss on him, too.

"Want to play, Krasaaveetsa?"

"Depends on what exactly that means, Tate." I lick up the side of his neck and he shivers, making a rumbling sound in his throat and it's so sexy.

"It means I get to feel that sweet cunt, wrapped tightly around my cock, little pet. I want to make you feel good again." I pull him between my legs and kiss him full on the mouth. He returns my kiss, fervently. I match his tongue with mine, softly caressing.

If he is any good at reading me, he will know this is not just a yes, but a hell yes. I am so ready for him. It's been sweet torture sleeping next to him every night this past week, feeling his hard body holding me tightly. I wrap my legs around his body and lightly drag my nails down his back.

He growls, "Ahhh, that's it, Krasaaveetsa, you're mine, baby."

He nips at my neck and slides his hands around my waist. He picks me up and I keep my legs wrapped around him, while I clutch onto his shoulders. Tate easily carries me about a foot away and sets me on the counter.

He pushes me backward so I'm leaning on my elbows. He looks so gorgeous, his cheeks are stained a slight crimson from being turned on, he's slightly panting and his hair is sticking out every which way from my hands running through it. He snakes both hands up each of my thighs, pushing the material of my loose, white sundress up until he gets to my lacey thong. He looks at me, his eyes dilating as he takes me in.

Tate starts murmuring in Russian and it shoots straight to my pussy, "YA praava, vee как maya krasaaveetsa, nafsegda (I claim you as mine beauty, forever)."

I sigh, "Mm, whatever you're saying, keep saying it. I love how it sounds."

My panties are soaked, each time he rasps something new in Russian, I get wetter. He smirks at me, sending me a look that says, 'if you only knew.' Tate leisurely pulls my thong down my legs and licks his bottom lip a little as he takes me in.

"Please, Tate, don't slow down, I want you so badly."

"Shh, baby, I know."

He starts with his fingers, pumping steadily inside me. *Holy fuck, does that feel good.* I tug on his hair, to let him know I want more. I just want him. I need to feel all of him deep inside of me. Tate lifts my dress up over my head and starts to kiss me all over. He starts at my tummy eagerly moving up to the tops of my breasts. I'm so glad I chose to wear matching panties and bra today. I want to look perfect for him.

"Oh! That feels so good," I gasp out.

He's so phenomenal at eliciting these amazing feelings coursing throughout my body. I place my hands on each side of his face and start to tug him up my body more. I don't want to wait any longer.

"Tate, no more waiting, I need to feel you inside me."

He peers into my eyes for a few seconds, almost as if he's reassuring himself that I really am ready for this. I grin encouragingly and bump his nose lightly with mine. It seems to shake him out of his thoughts and he peels off his shirt.

I run my hands down his smooth, cut body and then on the way back upward, lightly tug on his nipple rings. Sitting up, I draw his left nipple ring into my mouth. I use my tongue to play around with it, tugging with my teeth gently and flipping it back and forth with my tongue. I let it go slowly and look down the rest of his body. His cock is extremely hard, peeking out of the top of his pants. God, it's so erotic, I just want to lick it.

I whimper, "Can I lick it, Tate?" I keep my eyes on his straining dick so I don't see his expression.

"Fuck!"

He starts to shove his pants down forcefully. Good, he's going to let me take him in my mouth. I hope I do as good of a job as he does. I begin to slide off of the counter, to get onto my knees.

"Oh no, Krasaaveetsa, you can put my cock in your mouth later. Right now, I'm going to make that cunt all mine. Hold onto the side of the counter, this is going to be rough."

My pussy convulses at his words, eagerly awaiting his promise and I feel my wetness dripping down to my butt. Tate grasps my ankles, pulling me so that I slide to the edge of the counter. He kicks his pants the rest of the way off and I see him completely for the first time. Holy fuck he's big! His dick reaches up to his belly button. *That has to be at least eight inches.* No way will that fit in me. I look at him a little panicked and he answers my trepidation by grabbing the nape of my neck, kissing me passionately.

He grips my thigh in his other hand firmly, then moves the hand away from my nape, using it to pump his cock while he works it into me. Tate rubs the head in my wetness, drawing it up, all along my pussy lips. He parts my lips gently with his cock and then thrusts inside me deeply.

"Oh God!" I gasp at the fresh feel of pleasure and the pinch of pain accompanying it.

It's been awhile since I was with my ex. Two years actually and he doesn't hold a candle to Tate's size. I take a few deep breaths, relaxing my muscles. Tate won't hurt me purposefully. I trust him. I love him.

He murmurs close to my ear, comforting me, "Good girl, just relax and take me in, baby. It will fit I promise, especially with all your pussy juice leaking everywhere. You are so fucking beautiful like this, fuck, so beautiful."

It makes me burn up inside to hear him talk about my pussy juices leaking all around his cock. I hold on tight to the edge of the counter as Tate goes to town, thrusting hard into me. It feels as if it's a really tight fit, but no longer painful, just full.

Tate moves his fingers down between us and holds onto the base of his dick for a few seconds, as it goes in and out of me. He gets his fingers wet from it and then starts to rub light circles on my clit.

It feels out of this world, I'm building, I'm almost...*so close*...oh God I'm going to come.

"Oh my God, Tate, it feels fucking awesome, I'm going to fucking come, please, please, harder!"

"That's it, Emily, milk my cock. I'm going to fill you up so fucking full of my cum."

His voice vibrates through me and I explode at his words. I drag my nails down his back, digging in hard. I know it will leave marks. I lean in and bite his neck roughly, as I gasp his name out on the crest of my orgasm.

He hears my gasp "Tate" and his dick starts to pulse frantically inside of me. My pussy is so tight around him, I can feel each time his cock convulses. The warmth of each spurt of his cum, as he paints the inside of me is delicious.

After a few moments, he lays his big body over mine, resting on the kitchen counter for a few beats. His face is placed on my chest as he catches his breath. I relax, softly playing with his hair and close my eyes.

So this is what bliss feels like. I can't wait until we get to do that again, that's for sure. A chill runs over me after a minute and I shiver. The granite countertop is not made for warmth or comfort.

Tate must feel me because he stands back up, briefly bending over, placing a soft kiss on my lips and then my forehead. He lifts me up with him easily and carries me to his bedroom. I'm thinking round two, but am pleasantly surprised when he places me in the bathtub.

"Relax and get warm, baby." He smirks and winks, then turns and leaves the bathroom. Well, guess I'm taking a nice bath then. I don't mind that at all.

Sapphire Knight

Chapter 11

Emily

One week later...

I needed to come to my apartment to get some more stuff to take to Tate's. London and I never once imagined that we would be staying there for so long. It's going on three weeks now, when we were planning for the latest being one week.

The boys are stuck in class, taking tests that I've already completed, so London offered to come home with me. One of the perks of having Tate drive everywhere is we don't have a car. I consider it a perk since Tate is nice enough to let me use his Mercedes. He told me I could just have the whole freaking car. *Crazy man.* I told him no and instead of arguing back with me, he declared that we would go pick one out that I like. *Yeah right.* I'm not letting him buy me a damn car.

I also can't fathom that London is still here. I heard her and Cam arguing about her looking for a job last night in Cameron's room. It took everything I had not to interrupt them. I hate it when they fight, London deserves better than that.

"Hey chick, so, I was thinking, maybe you should just stay here. This semester's already halfway over anyhow. I mean, if you're planning on coming back to live here for next semester, it's silly to waste money on the back and forth traveling. You can still do your classes here on a computer, right?" I swiftly glance at her out of the corner of my eye as I drive. I'm a cautious driver; I always try to pay extra attention to everything around me.

"Well, um, about that--I kind of already finished all the assignments that were due for my classes and turned everything in. So now I just have to wait until the professor's grade all my work."

"Holy shit! That's great, London! You need to transfer here, you are way too freaking smart for those classes you take. You truly are the most intelligent person I know. I'm so proud of you, chickadee!" She nods, giving me her signature cocky smile.

"Thanks, you know, I am pretty great. But, so, yeah I was thinking if I liked it, I might just stay and have Mom send me some of my shit. I haven't done anything or shopped since you left, so I've saved literally every penny. I don't have a lot of money, but I have enough to pay for my first semester if I don't get picked up for a scholarship right away. I also received my acceptance letter before I came."

"That's great, I'm so happy for you! I bet Momma and Elliot are super proud of you for transferring to a university. Hey, we never did get to talk about why you showed up out of the blue with all the drama going on." Thinking of that shit brings a sick feeling to my stomach.

"Oh my God, I'm glad you brought that up. I completely got sidetracked, but I wanted to tell you as soon as I got here. You just looked so happy with Tate; I didn't want to ruin it right away."

"And what's up with Elliot? I've called and texted that jerk, a few times."

"Okay, so I guess the Sheriff went to your granddad's house to let you know Jeremy was getting released early. Well, Rosa, the lady who Elliot has to come clean, answered the door and got the message. According to Elliot, he didn't see her for like a week because of their schedules, and the dumb bitch didn't think to write the freaking message down!" She huffs, irritated. "So, when he finally saw her she gave him the message. He was so pissed, he freaked out and fired her. He showed up to Mom's house spazzing out about how I had to drive up here to warn you and make sure you were okay."

"Okay so why didn't he just call me, then?"

"I guess he had tried to call you and it went to voice mail. I told him you were probably locked in your apartment doing homework with your phone on silent. That is your usual routine. He got pissed believing that Jeremy had already gotten to you; he threw his phone and busted it all up. Then he took my car to the station, filled it up with gas and checked all the fluids while I packed my stuff. He tried calling you again from my phone and it still went to voice mail, so he and Mom shoved me in the car as quickly as possible and programmed my GPS. Elliot handed me a wad of cash saying he'd get a new phone later and sent me on my way with instructions to warn you. It was like nine o'clock at freaking night, so I drove all night long. I was so tired when I got here, but I realized I could catch you after your class. I'm so glad you had given me your schedule and sent me the campus info, because I had a map and was easily able to find where to go. That's probably why you thought I looked like a zombie when you saw me."

I shake my head at what she tells me. I don't doubt it at all, shit like that always seems to happen to her or her family. "Wow, that's crazy. I wish you would have told me when you first got here, though. We could have avoided some of this possibly. Geez, I had no idea. I even kept telling myself I needed to call you both more, but I just had so much homework that week before our long weekend. Then we kept playing phone tag. Fuck! I can't believe that freaking psycho is out loose somewhere."

"I know. I can't believe it either. Did Tate tell you about what he was screaming about outside when ass fuck wrote on the wall? Did I really hear him say Jeremy is fucking with the Mafia? I mean what is that all about? I asked Cameron but he won't say anything about it, just tells me it's none of my business."

"Shit, I was so upset, I honestly forgot he'd even said that. I'm going to talk to Tate about it."

We arrive at the apartment complex and drive all around to make sure there are no stalkers hiding out, waiting for me. I'm scared to go into my apartment now, but at least London's with me.

We park, making our way through the entryway and up to my apartment. I glance at her as I sluggishly unlock and open the door. "Oh, thank god, I was so nervous it was going to be trashed or something." I let out the breath I was holding and step inside.

Once we get completely inside, I survey the apartment and it appears as if everything is where it was when we cleaned it up before leaving a few weeks ago. "I'm going to jump in the shower really quick since I have my razor here. I have trees growing on my legs." I smile sheepishly.

"Gross, Em! Why didn't you just use Tate's razor? I used Cam's. He wants to touch me? Then he can lend me his razor."

"I don't know. I guess I don't want him to feel like I'm completely taking over his whole life."

"Please, that man is making you his whole life. Wake up, darlin', and smell the rich, fine-ass flowers in front of you. Since everything's kosher, I'm gonna go downstairs to the laundry and wash the dirty clothes we have here, while you shower and pack. Give me your front door key and I'll lock the door. Is that okay? Or if you want, I'll stay until you're finished."

"No, go, I'm fine. That's actually a great idea. Way to kill two birds with one stone." I wink, grabbing my key off the counter and hand it to her.

"We need to get you a key made; remind me later, after we have lunch. My bed is big enough for both of us, so we can share it until we can move to a two bedroom in the building, okay?" She grabs the key out of my hand and smacks a big, sloppy, wet kiss on my cheek.

"Sounds like a plan, cow, now get your hairy ass in the shower!" She takes off, running and laughing. She's lucky I love her or I would throw something at her.

"Cow?! Your ass is way bigger than mine!"

"Yeah, yeah." she hollers and walks to the bedroom. I shake my head; she's a dork.

I head into my bathroom and take a deep breath. I haven't been taking my anxiety pills while staying at Tate's and it seems to have cleared my head up more. I'm a little excited, but I think it's because I get to use all my own stuff.

Tate's home is beautiful and he's so giving, making sure I have what I ask for, but there is nothing quite like using your own stuff. My hair has definitely gotten spoiled though, using his salon shampoo and conditioner. It even smells good, like juniper.

I undress, toss my clothes in a pile on the floor and start the shower. After a few beats, I step into the steamy area. I relax under the hot spray and massage my neck with my fingers. My extracurricular activities with Tate have me a little sore in some spots. *Yum.* Speaking of Tate, I can't wait to find out what he will do to me later. That man is phenomenal with his hands, mouth and cock. I picture him naked in the shower, rubbing his strong hands all over his soapy body...

Wait, what was that? Oh, I bet it's just London coming for more laundry. I stand extra still and quiet my thoughts to listen—just to make sure. I'm probably being paranoid. I hear an almost silent click. *Nope, not paranoid.* That was a legit noise.

"London, what are you doing?" I shout, so she can hear me.

I wonder if she's having issues with the front door lock. I do sometimes, I know it's cheap. I don't get a response, so whatever, she must have figured it out. I go back to washing my body with my favorite Bath and Body Works body wash. It smells divine and makes me feel soft everywhere.

The hair on the back of my neck stands up when I feel a little breeze of cold air. The a/c is not on because I would be able to hear it humming. I feel the cool air caress me again and my insides start to jump. You know when you get the feeling that you want to look, but you really don't want to look? That's exactly how I feel. I swear if this is London fucking with me, I will wring her neck. The thing is, I know London likes to mess with me, but she's not cruel.

Deep inside my belly I know it's not her and it makes me nauseous. *Fuck!* I should have brought my gun in here with me. What an idiot! Have I not learned anything? My fears are confirmed when I hear his dark voice.

"I know you're finished, time to get out."

That's all it takes for me to go into a full-blown panic attack. Oh my god, my chest feels so tight and I can't breathe. Fuck! I have to make myself take deep breaths—

in...out...in...out...one...two...three...four...five...six...seven...eight...nine...in...out...in...out. I'm okay, I can handle this. I need to get to my room so I can get my pistol.

Jeremy rips open the shower curtain with a snarl. I see him for the first time since we were in that court room, two years ago. *He's gotten thinner.* He was already fairly thin before. Now it looks like every ounce of fat he had has melted off, and in its place is lean muscle. He must have spent his time working out the entire time he was in jail. Jeremy's hair is longer now, the midnight black locks now graze his shoulders and he has a few days' worth of scruff covering his face.

His face twists into an angry smirk and his eyes look at me with pure hatred. The little bits of softness I once saw in him are completely gone now. He reaches into the shower lightning quick and snatches my arm harshly, making me call out in fear, yanking me out of the shower so fast I stumble over the built-in bathtub.

"Ow! Please let go, Jeremy, I'll walk, please!" Fuck, my leg's killing me. I'm going to have a huge bruise from the damn tub. I hope he didn't sprain my ankle; it's on fire right now.

"You think I'm gonna be letting you go this time, bitch, so you can run again? I don't fucking think so."

His other hand grabs onto my wet hair to hold me, then he pulls his right leg back and lays into my thigh with a solid kick. *Holy fuck.* The breath is stolen from me and new tears crest in my eyes from the sharp pain. I'm not going to be able to walk. Please let London be okay, there's no telling what he did to her.

I choke, trembling. "Ouch! I-I'm so sorry. I promise I won't run, never again, okay? I promise, no running." I have to placate him with what he wants to hear, so he will calm down some. I have to get to my gun to get away from him.

"Boo, I know you won't go anywhere; you won't be leaving this fucking apartment."

Jeremy has a hold of me by my arm and my hair, dragging me forcefully toward my bedroom. It hurts so insanely bad, my scalp is screaming at me. If he doesn't let up soon he'll rip my hair out.

We finally make it to my bedroom, where he tsk, tsk, tsks at me, shaking his head. "You dumb, ignorant bitch, thinking you could leave *me* before I was done with you. Then you come here and start fucking somebody else? You always were a fucking whore, weren't you? I thought I took care of that issue, when I took care of that fucking thing in your stomach."

He throws me on my bed and I scramble as fast as I can to my nightstand. I may only have this chance to get to it.

Jeremy lets out a loud, deep belly laugh. "Oh, you thought I wouldn't search through your shit? You looking for something, boo? Go ahead and see if it's in there." He nods towards the little stand; I close my eyes and let the tears slip free. *He got my gun.* I reach into the drawer, under the book where it was hidden and feel it is definitely missing. I don't know what to do. I can't overpower him; I'm tiny and he's even stronger than before. I pray London stays downstairs. He has my gun so it wouldn't surprise me if he decided to kill her if he knows she's here; he hates her.

"Now, back to what I have planned. First off, I'm going to take what's owed to me. I'm glad you washed that fuck off you. Don't worry, I plan on killing him. He won't touch you again." I tightly clinch my eyes closed and put my head down. Please God no, not my Tate. I will do anything to save him. I can't let him get hurt. I love him too much...please God, I will do anything you want, just don't let my Tate get hurt.

I clear my throat, attempting to push down the pain that's radiating throughout my heart and body. "Forget about him, I don't want him. I will do whatever you want, Jeremy. I promise." I feel like I'm giving my soul to the devil, but I will sacrifice anything to save Tate.

The bedroom door flies open, crashing into the wall with a loud bang. I glance up quickly, stunned.

London stands in the doorway looking like a pissed off goddess. "Get the fuck away from her, you piece of shit!" she bellows, heatedly. *London! What the fuck—she has my gun?*

She waves the gun slightly. "Your stupid ass left this laying on the counter. Never were too smart, huh, J boy? Now get the fuck out," she grits. "I already called Tate, and he and his boys can't wait to get a hold of you!" London finishes with an evil looking grin and I can't help the little flutter of hope that appears in my belly.

Jeremy grabs me up, holding onto my arms and places me in front of him as a shield.

"Not smart huh, you fucking whore? You wanna shoot me; you have to shoot through her first. Now get outta my way, Emily and I are going to take a fun trip."

He starts to steer me out of the room. I can feel he's shaky. London backs up, keeping the gun trained on us, the entire trek to the living room. I'm so grateful for Granddaddy teaching us how to use different guns when we were growing up. I know London's not as good of a shot as I am, but if I can move at least half my body, I know she can clip him somewhere.

London smiles really big at him and my stomach drops. She's going to end up making him angrier and I'm not going be able to get out of his claw-like grip. This man feels like he has hands of steel with how hard he's gripping me to him.

I hear a choking sound and his grasp starts to loosen on my arms. A few moments later, Jeremy's hands fall completely away from me and I drop to the ground, finally free. I crawl to London as quickly as I can and she squats down. She tenderly pulls me into her arms and tightly hugs me to her. I peer over at where Jeremy was just holding me and I gasp.

Nikoli has his arm wrapped like a tight band around Jeremy's throat, in a choke hold. Jeremy's face is bright red and he's gasping, trying to catch any little breath. Good, that's how I felt when he touched me, like I couldn't breathe. Jeremy rakes his hands along Nikoli's strong forearm, but he is no match for the Russian beast's strength. Jeremy goes limp, his eyes closed and mouth wide open, almost as if he saw a ghost. I feel a semblance of relief inside that Jeremy looks like he's dead.

Nikoli drops Jeremy to the ground; he lands like a sack of potatoes. Niko grins down at Jeremy, "Oh man, The Boss is going to be so happy I finally caught you, you sneaky, little dude."

London escorts me to my room, helping me get a large t-shirt and some stretchy shorts on. I can't believe I was naked during that whole onslaught. I have carpet burn from Jeremy dragging me around, my scalp is extremely sore and I know my body is going to be littered with bruises.

After we finish in my room, Niko fills us in. Tate has had Nikoli show up at the apartment at random times ever since we left to stay with them, trying to catch Jeremy breaking in. Thank god for these men and their sly thinking, they probably just saved mine and London's lives. Niko has London run to his truck and get some rope out of the back to tie Jeremy up with.

He turns to me, with a sweet expression, "You okay, Tate's Krasaaveetsa?" Niko asks, while he has the gun now trained on Jeremy.

"You can just call me Emily if you want, Niko. Is he dead?" I gesture towards the lump on the floor. "Why do you have the gun still on him?" He smiles a little smile at me and then focuses back on his task.

"I call you The Boss' Krasaaveetsa, because that is what you are. You deserve respect, so I give it to you. And this moosar is not dead, just passed out."

"What is moosar?"

"It is trash, he is moosar."

"Yeah, definitely agree with you on that. Why do you call me Boss? Is Tate your boss? I thought he was your friend?"

"Yes, I do some work for him. He is my friend; he is moy braat (my brother)."

He glances away as if he is done talking, so I shut up. I really should take a Russian class so I can pick up some of these words they use. Whatever 'braat' means, Niko said it with great respect. I need to try to remember to look it up. I feel like a pest always asking them what stuff means.

London walks back in, looking tired and flustered with the rope in hand. Nikoli goes to work, tying Jeremy up in some complicated knot technique. I stand back to watch as London holds the gun for him.

Tate shows up about ten minutes later, appearing relieved when he sees me sitting on the couch.

"Krasaaveetsa, are you okay? Are you hurt? Thank God, Niko was here!" He rushes toward me and pulls me into his arms. Tate touches my arm where it's sore and I wince.

"Shit, baby! What is it?" He looks me all over, but can't see anything. Slowly, he runs his hand over the same spot, watching for my reaction to see where it hurts.

"Ouch," I draw my arm back, slightly, "you touched a spot where he grabbed me." Tate's nostrils flare angrily and he flexes his jaw.

I tell Tate everything about what happened and where I'm hurt. When I'm done, Nikoli informs him of the rest of the story from when he showed up. Tate looks furious.

Tate orders, "Load him up, Nikoli, and take him to Gizya's old storage building. Get my tools and the bleach ready, I'll be there as soon as I get Emily settled back home." Niko nods, looking excited. "I want his knees first when he wakes up, then I'm going to take him apart, piece by piece. Also get Viktor for clean-up tonight."

Nikoli nods, "Boss." He sets to doing what he's told; this is a side of Tate I'm not used to seeing. I've always known Tate was domineering and people seem to jump when he tells them to do something, but this is Tate in business mode.

Chapter 12

Cameron shows up toward the end to check on us. I think he was really there because he wanted to see how London was. He drives us back to the house in Tate's car, because we are way too much of a wreck right now for either London or I to drive it. I thought Cam was going to blow a gasket when he heard London had pulled a gun on Jeremy instead of waiting for help. There were lots of hushed, serious whispers going on between them.

The ride home is an uncomfortable silence; Cameron is looking angry and London just stares out the passenger window lost deep in her thoughts. I have no idea what's really going on with them, but I hope she confides in me soon. Tate said he was stopping to talk to his brother really quickly and would be right behind us. I guess Viktor has a house close to Tate's in a different posh neighborhood.

Once we arrive, we all shuffle into the house and Muffin greets me right away at the door. He brings a smile to my face, knowing he was anxiously waiting for me to return. I scratch his ears for a moment then make my way to the living room. He follows and we sit down on one of the plush couches. A few minutes of petting him relaxes me and gets my breathing back to normal finally. I never knew a dog could help with my anxiety.

A while later, I'm nudged awake. I dozed off once I finally relaxed with Muffin. I think it's just the dog, wanting me to scratch his ears again but glance up to find Tate, peering down at me with sad, worried eyes.

"Hi, moy Krasaaveetsa, how are you feeling?" he asks, his Russian undertone, thick with emotion. I blink a few times and process his question. I didn't even realize I fell asleep. This couch is so comfy; I keep sleeping on it every time I sit down. I yawn a huge yawn.

"Geez, I didn't know I was so sleepy or I would have just laid down in the bed. Umm, I'm okay, just sore all over. What's wrong handsome?" I don't like seeing him sad, I wish he would smile.

"Da, that's normal, it's from the adrenaline rush earlier. It sucks all your energy out. I brought you a chocolate bar to help get your sugar back up." He runs his hands through his hair. "What's wrong? Well, first off, I wasn't there to protect you. I promised you I would keep you safe." He shakes his head, annoyed. "I feel like such a damn failure. It breaks me to know you are hurt and I could have been there with you to help you." This man is the sweetest, most caring man I have ever met. What is he talking about, failing me? He's the reason I'm okay right now!

"Are you kidding me, Tate? If you hadn't had Nikoli checking the apartment periodically, I would probably be dead right now! Instead, I'm here next to you and I'm okay. Please, don't be upset. During this whole disaster, I realized something very important and I want to tell you." I gaze at him, slightly nervous until he nods, telling me to go on. "I realized that I'm in love with you, Tate. During all of that scary time at my apartment, I thought of how much I care about you and how I love you so much. I know it's quick and probably way too soon, I mean it's been what? Two months? But, I just can't help it."

I grip his hand tightly, hoping he can feel just a semblance of the warmth I have for him inside. "You helped me today, probably more than you realize. Tate, you helped me get through it during the ugly things he was saying to me and when he physically hurt me. Each time, I thought of you and it made my heart warm. Then you really did save me, by having Nikoli there. Trust me, things could have been so much worse. Let's just be happy that I'm sitting here—next to you—right now. Please."

He hesitates, a little unsure. "I care about you a lot, Krasaaveetsa, but there are a lot of things you don't know about me. I also have my own secrets. I don't know if you could handle everything about me." He glances away, looking at the floor for a few beats, then returns his glance to me. "I may be nice to you, but I'm not so much to others." He appears so serious when he says this and I hope in my heart things aren't so bad that I can't handle them.

"I think I can handle it, Tate. At least I hope so. You accept me with all of my problems and I want to be able to do the same for you. If it helps, I know you have the club and you're like Nikoli's boss. I know you have lots of money and your brother works in money. I heard your conversation earlier with Nikoli about what to do with Jeremy, so I know you're no Saint. Then there was when you yelled outside my apartment. Did you yell about the Mafia? Did I hear you right?"

"Let's start with what you heard me tell Niko to do. You do realize I wasn't just saying those things, right? I really do plan to do all of that to your ex. Can you live with that, Krasaaveetsa?"

I recall everything he said to Nikoli at my apartment. Those were some serious threats he implied and I know Jeremy will not come out of it alive. After all of the pain and suffering he put me through, can I live with myself or Tate knowing Jeremy is gone forever? That he will never hurt me again, never stalk me, and never take my babies away from me, ever again. *Yes, I can live with that.*

"Yes, Tate, I can deal with it. It may make me a bad person to say this, but I will actually breathe easier, knowing he's finally gone. I will finally be able to relax, knowing he can never hurt me again." I look him in the eyes and say it as sincerely as possible. Tate needs to know I'm completely serious about this.

"That's good, Krasaaveetsa, because I do indeed intend to kill him. It will be bloody and painful, and he will suffer a great deal for ever touching you." He sighs. "Now, about what I said in the parking lot at the apartments. What do you know about the Russkaya Mafiya, Krasaaveetsa, huh?"

"Um, well, not much. I think we studied about the Italian Mafia in school. Is it close to the same thing?"

"Eh," he shrugs a little, "I guess you could compare it to the Italians, but Russkaya work a little differently. Does the Mafiya scare you?"

"No, not really. But that's probably because I've never been around it before and I don't really know much of what they do, aside from some movies I've seen with London."

"Does it scare you to know I'm Mafiya?" He peers down at me questionably and I shrug, unsure.

"My father, Gizya, is The Big Boss here in America. It means he is in charge of everyone, the entire thing. That's around five thousand people, Krasaaveetsa. I may not be The Big Boss yet, but I am a Boss. People do answer to me, and I do a lot of business for my father and uncle." I nod, taking it all in.

"Who's your uncle? Have I met him yet?"

"No, you have not. You shouldn't meet him unless we decide to marry. He's another type of Boss." My eyes widen at the marriage part and he smirks, continuing on. "My uncle is second in command here, in the Solntsevskaya Bratva. They are like us too, but more of a criminal element. They take care of the really bad stuff. I try to keep our businesses on the cleaner side of the law."

"That's not so bad then," I cut in and he shakes his head.

"Don't mistake, I do also partake in an array of bad things. I do kill bad people and make a lot of decisions you would not agree with." I swallow a large gulp when he talks about killing people so nonchalantly. "I need to know if this scares and upsets you, baby. I will not put you through this if you are not one hundred percent up for it. I will not keep you if you are scared of me and of my business." He looks completely serious and I believe him. I also trust that he would never purposely put me in any type of danger.

"Okay, I trust you, Tate. It's pretty frightening, but I know you would never get me hurt and you would keep me safe if anything were to happen. Is umm, all of your family in the Mafia?"

How will I fit into his life if I am not like them? Will his family even like me? The thoughts of his family are more overwhelming to me, than the whole Mafia thing.

"Yes, my family is Mafiya. We've covered the basics now and we will talk more about this later, Krasaaveetsa. Right now I have business to take care of." He stands up from the couch and I sit up.

"By business, you mean Jeremy, right?" I don't know if I really want to know the answer to my question, but I ask it anyway.

"Look, I won't be informing you about my business or anything to do with my Mafiya stuff. I don't want to taint you with the gruesome details of my dealings. I will tell you right now though about this, yes, it is about Jeremy. I'm only informing you because it has to do with you directly."

"I understand part of your life has to be private, but we are definitely not done discussing this. I want to know as much as you can tell me. I'd also like to know how all this will affect me being with you."

"Agreed, Krasaaveetsa, I will tell you what I can. God, baby, you have made me a very happy man today." He kisses me roughly and I can tell he's excited. I'm so happy he's not sad anymore. I hated to see him so upset, it hurt my heart.

He didn't seem freaked out earlier when I told him how I feel either. I didn't say it to him so he would automatically say it back, but I can't help but wonder just how he really feels about me. Once he leaves, I head to his bedroom. Soaking in the tub for a while, I play the day over in my head again. Everything that happened, everything that I learned, it was pure overload.

I turn the water on hot, to help my muscles relax, eating the delicious Hershey's chocolate bar. I accompany the chocolate with a glass of sweet wine and I think of how lucky I am. When I came here a few months ago, I never would have guessed to meet such supportive people. For the first time since I arrived at Tate's house, I go to bed alone and I hate the feeling.

Tate didn't come home until after I was asleep last night. I heard the shower come on and then a while later I felt him crawl into bed. He pulled me close to him and kissed the back of my head. I fell back asleep comfortable, warm, happy and content.

***

The next day, we all have class with completely different schedules, so everyone misses each other at the house. Tate woke me up with a nice surprise. He had rolled me over onto my belly and worked some of his frustration out on my pussy. He wasn't the only one who enjoyed it. I came twice and was trying to jump him again, before he crawled out of bed. I hope we aren't too loud; I don't want anybody else to hear us. I never thought of it before, but anyone could have walked into the kitchen the other day when he took me on the counter. I haven't heard anyone else in the house though, so I think it's safe to say the walls are thick.

I wonder if London will want to have lunch today. I need to find out what's going on with her and Cameron. My phone beeps with a text. It's my handsome man.

T – Baby, don't make plans for dinner. We're going to my parents' house.

Me – What?! You can't just spring this on me right now! Dinner's in a few hours!

I'm going to strangle that man. He wants to have dinner with his parents and I know absolutely nothing about them, besides that they are part of the mafia. I also have nothing nice to wear. Oh my God, they will probably think I'm some hussy after Tate's money or something crazy.

T – Yes, baby. Be ready at 7. I'll switch out cars then and we can go.

Me – Okay, but you so owe me for this!

T – Whatever you want, Kapacota <3

Me – TTYS Sugar Dimples <3

Aw he sent me a heart! He's so sweet sometimes. I follow up with sending London a text. Hopefully she's not with Cam, so she can help me find something to wear.

Me – 911 woman, I need you to help me find something NICE, not slutty, to wear to Tate's parents for dinner tonight.

I look up from my phone when I hear her voice, "Seriously, lazy ass, you couldn't walk down the hallway to Cam's room and ask me in person?" She's wearing a cocky smirk.

London has on one of Cameron's white undershirts and a pair of his boxers. He would probably scold her if he saw her so informal walking around the house, but she totally looks hot in it. He seems to like to keep London in check. I think it's good for her, considering she's normally a total wild child. She has her hair pinned on top of her head in a messy bun and is sucking on a Blow Pop.

"I didn't know you were in his room or I would have. What are you doing?" I gesture to her comfy outfit. "You look like a total bum, are you guys staying in tonight?" She shrugs and looks a little bored.

London shrugs, pouting. "Eh, he has stuff to do so I'm just hanging out and doing laundry. I might head to that little pastry shop right outside the neighborhood and get a pastry and coffee. I don't know, it depends if I decide to get dressed or not." She looks really bummed out now. I pat the spot beside me on the bed and she comes and sits next to me.

"Is everything going okay with you and Cameron? Y'all just jumped into it. I wasn't sure if this was just a fling or if you really like him." I take her hand in mine to offer her comfort and my attention.

"I know, I thought it was going to be a one-night stand type of deal, then after that night maybe two nights. He kept right on me ever since we first met and went out that night to the club." She rolls her eyes, "I told him about you going to Tate's parents and he thought it was too soon. I mean, I know you've been seeing Tate longer than me and Cam have been, but it's like the thought of me meeting his family never once crossed his mind. That hurt my feelings so I told him I thought you guys were crazy and I prefer to do my own thing. After that he looked pissed off and told me he had shit to do. He stormed out, saying he'd be back whenever he was done. So I have no idea what's going on right now. I usually never even give guys this kind of chance, but I'm a little addicted to Cameron right now. I just don't want to be that girl who nags, you know?"

Aww, my poor London. That sucks. It sounds like Cam was being a dick but who knows, I wasn't there to see how it all went down. I won't tell London that, though.

"That's really shitty, London, I'm sorry you are dealing with that right now." I hug her and rub her back for a second.

"I'm okay, you know I'm not one to put up with any shit when it comes down to it. Now, let's find you something awesome to wow the future in-laws. I'm excited for you!"

"In-laws, yeah right, they will probably think I'm a hussy after Tate's money with my luck." I huff, getting up and walking to the closet. Tate has unpacked my bags and moved all of my belongings into it. He just randomly did it without even asking me. I was pretty amused when I discovered it.

"Oh no, I'm pretty sure they will know what this means. Tate's what, like, twenty-two years old? And Cameron was saying that Tate has never introduced a female to his parents or family, like ever. So relax, they will know you are the real deal." London smiles big at me like this is the greatest news.

"Holy shit! This is even more horrible! Now, I know they will hate me! His dad will probably have one of his guys sink me to the bottom of a lake somewhere with cement blocks around my feet!"

She bursts out laughing at my descriptive picture and I just glare at her. If my leg still wasn't so sore I'd leap at her ass. She smirks at me and shakes her head; bitch knows me too well to know exactly what I'm thinking.

An hour later and plenty of amusing quips from London and I'm dressed. I'm in my white, baby doll style sundress, that's trimmed out in lace along the breast line and the bottom. I pair it with some cute white wedge sandals that Avery had packed in with her stuff.

Thankfully, Avery has smaller feet than London so I can borrow her stuff. We figured white was the virginal color, so hopefully his mom will approve. It's also the longest sundress I own. I'm shooting for modesty and good girl look. I think we've pretty much nailed it.

I leave my hair down and put a few curls in it. Not too fancy, but at least it looks like I tried with my appearance. I brush on some black mascara to accent my long eyelashes, a dust of blush along my cheek bones and smooth on some lip gloss. London sprays me down with my Heavenly perfume by Victoria's Secret and I'm all set.

It all worked out with perfect timing too because it is now 6:30 and Tate just pulled up to the house. Muffin runs to the front door at full speed and is jumping around whining, waiting for his dad to get inside.

Tate steps inside and he looks absolutely gorgeous. He's wearing a light grey button up shirt and some black slacks that mold to his physique perfectly. He looks professional and sexy but not overdressed. Muffin takes up his attention for a few minutes, wagging his butt around and nosing Tate to pet him. I love that he cares so much for his dog. Muffin is such a good boy. He has definitely stolen part of my heart, too.

Tate looks up and his sparkling hazel eyes take me in before they meet my green ones. "Damn, little lamb, you look breathtaking."

His eyes dilate as he walks toward me. He bends his head down and kisses me on my lips, soft and sweet, while he wraps his arms around me and pulls me into his solid chest. He whispers, "Fuck, I love coming home to you. I meant it this morning when I told you I want you to stay here." Wow, I thought that was just the sex haze talking when he said that earlier.

"I love being here too, Tate, but I also have London to think of. I can't just leave her when she's here for me." I wrap my arms around his neck and

155

pepper little kisses all over his jawline leaving little traces of my lip gloss. It's okay, I know he doesn't mind it.

"Then I'll tell Cam to keep her, too." He shrugs, saying this like it's the simplest answer and that Cameron will just keep seeing London, like it's not their own relationship or anything.

"No, Tate, I will talk to London about what she wants to do first, and then we can talk more about it, okay?" He answers me with a cheeky smile, the answer pacifying him for the time being and he twirls me around.

"Alright, let's go to my parents' house, Krasaaveetsa."

I grab my small purse and head to the garage to get into Tate's grey, Bentley Continental GT Speed. I broke down and asked him what it was called. *God, I fucking love this car!*

Tate pulls out of the garage, heading for the main road. "This car is my favorite, sugar dimples. I love how it sucks me back into my seat when you go fast." I smirk at him and put my seatbelt on. He starts to laugh and it lights up his whole face. Gosh, he's handsome.

"I am glad you like her, she is a good car. Would you like to drive her later? Perhaps on the way back?" He leans over, quickly kissing the tip of my nose and I sigh. He's freaking perfect and I'm the lucky one who has him.

"Maybe some time, but tonight I want to just sit back and watch you drive her. You look so sexy when you drive."

"Sexy, huh?" He gives me a cocky grin and I swat at his arm. I relax into the butter soft leather seat and watch the pretty scenery of Knoxville turn into the beautiful scenery of Tellico Lake, where his parents live.

Now, that was a great drive. Thirty miles of highway and his car got to really spread her wings. It felt like we flew, the drive was so comfortable and smooth. Tate's parents live in a very upscale, gated neighborhood full of mini mansions looking over the lake.

We pull up to a huge house that looks like a small castle made out of tan stone. The yard has a large circular driveway that is lit up and there is a beautiful pond off to the side, at the front of the house. On the opposite side of the house, there are trees and a beautiful wooden pergola with outdoor seating. The house is on just enough of a hill that when you look past the pond you can see a gorgeous view of the lake. I bet the view is even better on the second floor of the house or from the back yard.

Tate gets out, coming around the car and opens my car door. He takes my hand tenderly, to help me get out. While I'm climbing out and attempting to straighten my dress, the front door opens and a tall, lean man walks outside.

He chortles amused, to Tate, "I had to come see for myself if you really brought a date to dinner, moy braat Luka." When the man finally gets near us, I recognize it's his brother, Viktor, from the club.

"She's kraaseevee (beautiful), huh?" he says to Tate, gesturing towards me. Viktor turns toward me, giving me a wink. I have no idea what he called me but hopefully it wasn't fish food.

"Da, braat, she's moy Krasaaveetsa," Tate grumbles to his brother and then glances at me.

"I'm sorry to be so rude, baby. This is my brother, Viktor, the one I was telling you about."

I put my hand out to shake formally and he laughs at it. "Hi, Viktor. It's very nice to meet you." I mumble and peer at him confused; I don't know what's so funny.

"No, no, no, Luka's Krasaaveetsa." He pulls me to him and gives me a hug.

Tate smirks, so this must be good. I awkwardly pat his back a few times, and then pull away. Tate comes closer, resting his arm around me and I can feel myself start blushing.

"Oh, Krasaaveetsa, Atyets (beauty, father) will eat you up!" He grins wolfishly, "Atyets will love this, Luka. This is what he needs right now, to see you find someone. And such a Krasaaveetsa at that! Christ, your children will be absolute angels!"

Holy fuck! Did he just say our children? I haven't even made it in the front door yet. Oh no, I wonder if Tate has a crazy family. I bet that is going to be where all his flaws lay. I'm kind of scared to meet this 'Atyets' person. I let Tate lead, entering into the house first. I'm scared to let go of him or they might try to start breeding me before we even sit down to dinner.

I'm instantly astounded. The inside of Tate's parents' house is like nothing I've ever seen before. It's decorated in rich colors and golds. Everything implies wealth and it almost feels as if it's never used, it's very sterile. I get the whole 'museum' vibe from it.

There is one thing that I love as soon as I see it, though. On a side table there are these little, round doll things of all different sizes. They are each beautiful, artistically painted in a variety of colors and don't appear as if they really belong in this room.

A loud voice booms with a strong Russian accent, interrupting my thoughts. "Those are called Babushka, printyessa." I jump at the sound, Tate chuckling at me quietly. He shifts us so that we're facing towards his father.

Konstantin walks to us with his arms spread wide open. I'm assuming it's his father anyhow. He's a very good looking man, with stunning features, resembling Tate quite closely. He's in his mid-fifties I'd say.

Tate walks into his father's arms and they embrace each other. "Atyets," Tate states and kisses his dad's cheek. Konstantin returns the gesture, kissing Tate's cheek and responds, "Sin(son)."

His father then turns to me and pulls me in for a hug and in a strong Russian accent says, "And you, printyessa, you call me Papa, da (yes)? His smile is dazzling and it reminds me of one of my favorite things about Tate. Once he releases me from his tight embrace, I grin and nod.

"Come, my son and his Krasaaveetsa, let us get vodka and sit for dinner. Viktor, join us!"

I follow the three men who are all well over six feet tall. They make me feel like a dwarf next to all of them. We end up in a bar area that's richly decorated in wood so dark it almost appears black. The floor is large slabs of travertine in a pale grey color. The walls are decorated with many, large paintings of deer, bears and other animals you hunt. It's like a rich man's trophy room of sorts and there is a very pretty blonde lady, who is most likely his mother, sitting on one of the cocktail chairs.

She glares at me, sniffing in my direction with distaste. She turns to Tate, raises her nose and in an entitled voice reeking full of venom asks, "What is this, Luka Tatkiv?" She shoos her hand in my direction, "Why you bring a woman here, to my house?"

Tate huffs, "Mother, she is my Krasaaveetsa. I brought Emily to meet my family and have dinner." He squeezes my hand reassuringly and gives me a small smile. I squeeze back. *I'm okay right now.*

Vivi annoyingly grunts, "Luka, if it is time for you to marry, we will send you to Mother Russia. You get good Russian girl to be your bride. They will know how to take care of you and stay out of your businesses." She glares spitefully at me the entire time she says this and Viktor laughs loudly. I feel tears burning behind my eyes, but I refuse to let my eyes fill with them.

"Enough Vivi!" Konstantin roars at her. "My son brings his Krasaaveetsa home to meet his family, you shut up, shut up, shut up! You treat printyessa as family, she is my daughter now!" He declares. We all stay silent— including Vivi—after Konstantin's little outburst.

"Now we eat zazhaareets (roast) and enjoy a good vodka. Come," he orders a few moments later and we all fall-in to follow him to the formal dining room.

I smirk to myself, I like Tate's dad even more after that. I wasn't expecting it to be easy by any means to meet his family, but for his mom to say that shit? That Tate should find someone else all because I'm not Russian, makes me boil with anger inside.

To say dinner is awkward is an understatement. We all sit at this humongous, beautifully carved wooden table in the dining room that can seat twenty-two people. Who on earth has that many people for dinner? That's what BBQ's are for. A little, old Russian woman, they call Mishka, serves us ice water and a variety of three chilled tumblers, with a different vodka in each. If they keep this up, I'm not going to be able to walk. Thank God there's food! Speaking of, whatever we are having smells amazing.

Not too much later, Mishka wheels a shiny silver cart out and puts what appears to be a giant roast on the table. There are a couple other hand painted, delicate china bowls that have a variety of sides filling them to the tops, but I have no clue what they are. It all looks and smells amazing.

"Printyessa, you like zazhaareets (roast)?" Konstantin grins as he inquires. I bet Tate's dad is a lady killer with that smile.

I nervously giggle a little. "Well sir, I'm not sure what that is exactly, but this food smells remarkable!" I beam a bright smile back and hope he was referring to the food and not my ovaries or something.

Nodding approvingly, "Yes, Mishka is a very good cook. Please eat and enjoy." I dig in hungrily and I think it's the best food I've ever tasted.

"Luka, did you tell printyessa about what it is we do?" Konstantin gazes over at Tate. I would expect Tate to shy away from this question since the Mafia is so secretive.

"Da, I did. We had a complication arise and a few things were revealed. Emily is smart and figured some of it out before I was able to explain." Tate glances at me proudly.

"I hope no business complication? Did you need assistance? Or is this the old boyfriend problem? Nikoli handled it, da?" His dad peppers him with questions and it surprises me they are openly discussing this in front of me, over dinner no less.

"Nine (no), the businesses are good. Da, it has been handled, although I handled this case personally. Da, it was the ex. You heard?" His father chuckles when Tate says he handled it personally.

"Ahh, my Luka, the infamous 'Knees'. Am I right, moy sin, you took out his knees first?"

Konstantin seems to soak up immense joy in hearing about Tate being violent. It's like he's very proud of the fact that his son is called 'Knees'. *Is that even a name?* I have to talk to Tate about this later.

Tate grins and nods in agreement. Viktor starts laughing when Tate nods.

"You see, little printyessa, it is funny to us because the whole time Luka was growing up, if he got into a fight he went for the person's legs and broke their knees. We thought the poor boy didn't know how to defend himself. Turns out, he was incapacitating his opponents. Very smart, my son is. As he got older, he got more and more creative in breaking knees and eventually was honored with the name 'Knees.' You go to Russia and everyone knows who The Boss is that is named 'Knees.' You grow up fast in the life of a Boss."

I smile at him and hold my breath. Hearing about Tate breaking people's bones growing up, is not my idea of dinnertime conversation. I just have to make it through this meal and hopefully things will get easier with his parents, with time.

Konstantin bellows suddenly, "Mishka, the торт (dessert)!" I jump in my seat and Tate looks over at me like I'm the crazy one. I shrug and check around for Mishka. She comes walking in unhurriedly, with a huge cake covered in strawberries and a creamy sauce.

"Oh God, it looks so good, and if it's anything like dinner then she needs to just put the whole cake on my plate!" I burst excitedly, not realizing I just said it all out loud.

Everyone laughs loudly and Mishka looks at me with a smile for the first time. I guess she likes the compliment. Tate's mom even giggles slightly and her expression toward me seems to begin to thaw. I don't know if it's because I made her laugh, or if it's because of Mishka's reaction.

Dessert is considerably less awkward and I find myself really enjoying the evening. Konstantin boasted about different stories of the boys growing up and what Russia is like. You can tell that he is extremely proud of the men that his sons have become.

Vivi chimed in a few times with little details. I'm just happy to see her replace the nasty glare with a smile full of fond memories. I was seriously thinking I was going to have to hide all the knives for dinner; luckily she heeded Konstantin's advice and was polite throughout.

Konstantin shared that they try to spend Christmas at their country house, close to Moscow every year. He said that if the weather permits, then I will get to come with Tate in a few months. I glance at Tate to catalog his feelings about it and he appears really excited at the prospect of me spending Christmas with him.

We eventually finish eating and visiting. I thank Vivi and Konstantin numerous times for having me as a guest. I butter up Vivi with compliments about the food and house, and it seems to break through her shell a little more with each one.

Konstantin leads us to the front door once Tate declares that we are tired and leaving. Vivi embraces me in the foyer and in a strong, feminine, Russian accent she says, "Little Emily you must join me for lunch, we have much planning to do."

I smile, hugging her in return. "That sounds wonderful, Vivi, I look forward to it."

As soon as she lets me go, Konstantin squishes me in a strong hug. "Little printyessa, you must come pick a Babushka to take with you home." He beams happily and leads me toward the table.

"Oh no! I couldn't, they are so beautiful, but thank you." I look over at Tate and he nods at me, like 'yes, take one.'

"Da! I insist, please."

I stare at the Babushkas for a few beats. They are all so beautiful and appear very expensive. I reach out and run my hand over a smaller one that is painted bright blue. This one would look so pretty next to my bed.

"Good choice, printyessa! Now, go keep moy sin company and he must bring you back many times!" Tate cuts in by saying his goodbyes.

Viktor walks out with us. When we arrive at the car, Viktor opens my door for me and gives me a chaste kiss on the cheek.

"Good night, Saystraa (sister)."

I smirk back at him. "Good night, Viktor."

"Braat!" Viktor calls across the car and Tate gives him a fake salute before climbing in beside me.

My door closes and I'm left alone with Tate for the first time in three hours. I can't believe we were here for that long. The time just flew by once his dad started in on his stories.

"My family loves you, Krasaaveetsa." He looks like he's glowing, he's so happy.

"Yeah, I wouldn't go that far. I do like your family a lot though. Your mother is so lovely when she finally warms up and Mishka's cooking was out of this world!"

"Oh, no? You don't think so? My mother just invited you to a private lunch because she wants to plan a wedding for us, baby. The Babushka my father insisted you have is a fertility doll. My brother just kissed your cheek and called you 'little sister.' I'm pretty confident that they loved you tonight."

Tate chuckles, shaking his head. "My mother would have spit in your face if she didn't like you and my father would have called my Uncle Victor." Well shit. I guess I did okay after all. I'm glad to be on the Mafia king and queen's good side, that's for sure. His mother would have spit? And to think I almost cried when she said I wasn't good enough since I'm not Russian. What a crazy night, I can't wait to tell Avery and London all about this.

"Wow, that's just a tad bit overwhelming! I can't imagine your mom spitting, maybe scratching my eyes out. I'll tell you what though, if I keep eating Mishka's cooking I'll get fat! Then your dad will get his hopes up with that Babushka. That food was so fantastic!" He glances over at me, grinning as he drives.

"Yes, Mishka is a great cook. She is my grandmother and she taught me how to cook."

"What, your gram? Why didn't she sit with us then?"

"Mishka just prefers to cook, she is 'old Russian.' They did things differently back then. She cooks and she serves. She likes to take care of everyone and just observe. That lady is sneaky; she hears and witnesses everything. If anyone has a secret or some news to share, she always knows before everyone else does. When you talked about her cooking we laughed because we knew you had just won her. My mom had to give in; she'd never stand a chance if Mishka likes you."

"Oh man, that is awesome! I wonder if my gram would be like that if she were here."

I get sad inside and my heart squeezes.

"You didn't know your grandmother, Krasaaveetsa?"

"No, I don't remember her at all. She died from cancer when I was a year old. From what I've heard though, she was really protective and liked to help people in trouble. I hope I have some of that goodness in me, too."

"You are full of goodness and beauty, little pet, don't worry. She would be so proud if she were here today." I shoot Tate a small smile and squeeze his forearm. I love him. I do, so much.

Suddenly, I'm jerked roughly in my seat, my eyes grow wide and my head flies into the dash. My head bounces off the hard surface and everything goes black.

Chapter 13

Two days later...

I awake disoriented, to a pounding headache and beeping. I feel as though my body has been run over by a bus. The sheets are cold and scratchy. I have goose bumps adorning my skin everywhere and I feel miserably cold all over. Why do I feel so cold? And what is that damn beeping?

I open my eyes, fluttering them a few times as if I've been asleep for longer than usual. The florescent lights blaring down on me, seem extra bright. I rub my face a few times and something pinches my hand. Finally I can focus. I glance down and there's a needle and tube connected to my hand. I take a deep breath and look around.

I'm in the hospital. *Fuck, why am I in the hospital? Did Jeremy do this?* I check my body over and notice there aren't really any bruises or anything remarkably different that stands out. I don't think it was him. Oh God, in fact I know it wasn't him. Tate! Tate had gotten Jeremy. So why am I here?

I gaze all around, noticing that it's a private room and I'm all alone. It looks like a freaking florist in here. There are roses of all colors, in different arrangements on the little table in front of my bed. Beside my bed, there is another smaller table. It has a stuffed animal that looks a lot like Muffin. There's also a pitcher and a plastic cup. I'm assuming that it's water. *Thank God*, I feel like I could drink a gallon right now.

I attempt to reach for the cup but the movement shoots sparks of pain through my whole body, "Ouch!" I yip, and sit as still as possible.

Come on...really? I'm dying of thirst here. Ugh and my head is pounding so much. I reach up to rub it and feel I have something wrapped around my forehead. *What the fuck?*

The door to my room opens and I glance toward it. In walks Tate, he's busy looking at the ground and hasn't noticed me staring at him. A tear runs down his cheek and he wipes it away quickly.

I choke all raspy, "Baby?" Tate's head snaps up; once he sees my eyes are open, he runs to my side.

"Moy Krasaaveetsa! Oh, thank God, you have finally awoken! I've been going crazy!" Tate runs his hands through his hair grasping the ends tightly. He sits down on the side of my uncomfortable hospital bed and lightly gives me a peck on the lips.

"Water, please?" I rasp out. Geez, my throat is so sore and dry, and I sound like a chain smoker.

"Of course. How are you feeling, are you in pain?" Tate peppers off questions and hands me a paper cup, half full of water. I drink the cool, refreshing liquid quickly. This brings a small smile to his face. I barely nod at the pitcher and he fills my cup again. I drink it down swiftly again, famished.

"Ugh, thanks." I clear my throat a few times. "I hurt when I tried to move and get my own water. Why am I here?" I ask still confused and direct all of my attention to him.

He tilts his head quizzically, "You remember nothing?"

"No, I don't and what do you mean I finally woke up? How long has it been?"

"Fuck, Krasaaveetsa, it's been two long days that you've been sleeping. The doctors said it was because your body was healing and also because of the strong painkillers, but I've been going fucking mad inside wanting you to wake."

"Wow! Two days? What happened, Tate? The last thing I can remember, is telling your brother good night. I don't understand, what's wrong with me?"

"Shh, calm down, baby. Nothing's wrong, pet, you just hit your head really badly and had to get stitches on your forehead next to your hair."

He turns my palm over carefully, showing me all the cuts up and down my arm, glancing over I notice a few gashes in my other arm as well. "Then there was the glass that went everywhere; you got cut up fairly good in a few places from that also."

"My head is really foggy feeling and my body hurts." I whisper and pout a little. It hurts so badly, but I don't want to worry him even more.

"The doctor said the impact will probably give you whiplash in your neck, and your back will hurt for a few weeks. He said you are lucky to be so tiny because the car swallowed you up and protected you."

"How did it protect me if I was knocked out for a few days? I mean look at me, Tate, I'm covered in marks."

"Well, he said a bigger guy like me probably would have died in the passenger side. I was so scared. You were knocked out and unresponsive. I thought I had lost you."

"God Tate, I'm so glad it was me sitting there and not you. Thank God I refused to drive your car."

"No baby, just no. I wish none of this happened to you. I can't bear to see you hurt like this, it fucking guts me, Krasaaveetsa."

"I'll be okay Tate, we're fortunate to both be sitting here it sounds like."

"The fool who hit us in her car, is also in the hospital. She almost died because she hit us so hard. Stupid bitch," he hisses angrily. "The cops said she was drinking heavily and the alcohol helped relax her body." Tate looks so livid when he starts to talk about the other person. His eyes grow hard and his forehead gets a wrinkle in the middle.

Squeezing his hand, I attempt to distract him, so he will look at me and quit thinking whatever thoughts have him so angry. He gazes at me and a few tears begin to stream down his cheeks. It literally feels like my heart is squeezing painfully to see him like this.

"Please, Tate, I'm okay. I'm right here and you're here, and we're both going to be just fine."

"You just don't know, Krasaaveetsa," he murmurs, choked up, "I thought you were gone and I just found you. I haven't had enough time for something to happen to you. I'm a selfish man, Krasaaveetsa, and I refuse to wait."

He sits up with renewed focus. "I love you, beauty. I love you so damn much with all of me. I will give you everything of mine and anything I can in life to make you happy. Please agree that when you get better you will live with me permanently and that you will stay with me forever." I smile softly at the words I have been longing to hear ever since I confessed my feelings to him.

"Let me take care of you and cherish you. Let me marry you and give you lots of babies?" Tears continue to roll down his face, he grins slightly as he finishes, talking about babies. Happiness washes over me, filling me so full that I could burst and I fall deeper in love with him.

"Yes, of course Tate. I will stay with you, I promise. I love you so very much, too." He breaks out in a giant, pleased smile and gently peppers sweet kisses all over my face.

"My little love, you make me the happiest man in the world. I will take good care of you and love you always."

Savoring each of his words, I relish in the fantastic feelings they give me, while I rub my hand on his unshaven face. I take a really good look at him, coming out of my fog a little more with time and notice he looks a mess.

My Tate is always so well put together. This man beside me is a wreck; he looks like he's been through hell and back. His face is really scruffy; he has dark purplish bags under his eyes, and even they are red rimmed from his tears and lack of sleep. It appears as if he hasn't showered in days. Tate's in his white undershirt and a pair of dress pants; they are wrinkled and it's not something he would normally wear.

"Hey, sugar dimples, what are you wearing?" I look at him crazy and he starts to laugh. Ah, there's my Tate.

"I haven't been home since the wreck. This is my undershirt and the pants I had on at dinner with my parents." My God, my poor man.

"Oh, Tate," I shoot him a sad look. "Please go take a shower, put some clean clothes on, eat and take a nap. I'm okay now and I'm wide awake. You need to go and take care of yourself also."

"I'll call Cam and let him know to tell the girls you're okay and to bring me some clothes." He gestures around the room. "We're in a private suite, so I can just use the shower in here. Avery and London have been going nuts that you haven't been awake, also. I told them both that as soon as you woke up, I'd call them so they can come see you. They were worried sick about you." He pulls his phone out of his pocket and starts scrolling through his contacts. "I have to let my parents know also. I know Mishka will want to send you something to eat, so you aren't stuck eating hospital food."

"Okay, sweets, that sounds good. I would love some food from Mishka if she wants to make it." I whisper quietly. My head and throat are still hurting, along with every other single body part it seems. I hope London and Avery aren't really too upset. I'll never hear the end of how they were so worried about me and it'll make me feel super guilty.

"Will you please ask London or Avery to grab my iPod and Kindle so I can read and listen to music, when I feel better?"

"Of course, Krasaaveetsa, anything you want." *Wow.* That's definitely the right answer. I can't wait to jump his bones when I get out of here and no longer hurt.

Three days later...

"Oh my God, Tate! Get me out of here! I can't stay in this freaking uncomfortable bed, any longer. It's hard and making my butt go numb. At least take me home so I can see Muffin and be surrounded by my friends." I plead, and Tate rolls his eyes at me, exasperated. I've been attempting this all day and I think he's close to his breaking point.

"Krasaaveetsa, the doctor said you need to stay a few days still, just be patient. It's for your health."

I huff, "Tate, either you bust me out of here or I'm signing myself out and calling London."

"Alright, you win. It's been a few days since he said that, so I'll tell him you are ready to go and see what he says, okay?" I roll my eyes at him and he sticks his tongue out at me.

"I don't care what he says, I'm outta here!" I call out, teasing Tate. Finally, I break through to this stubborn man. I blow him kisses as he walks out. "Hate that you're leaving, but I sure do love watching you go!" I chortle, smiling cheekily and winking at him, this time it's him who rolls his eyes at me. He's so freaking cute, I just love him.

About thirty minutes later the door to my hospital suite opens, with Tate and Dr. Hopkins coming in.

"Hello, Miss Emily. I hear you are ready to leave us?" He smirks and his old eyes twinkle.

My doctor has to be pushing sixty years old, if not older. Tate says he's the best at this hospital and that's why he's assigned to me. He has a head full of white, fluffy hair and big green eyes. Dr. Hopkins looks like he's in good shape for his age but may have eaten a few too many bowls of chocolate pudding from the cafeteria.

"Yes, sir, I'm ready to blow this popsicle stand!" He starts chuckling and Tate shakes his head in exasperation.

I guess you can say I've been quite entertaining to the staff here while on my pain medication. I had to be or I would have gone out of my mind. Now all of the nurses have started calling Tate 'Sugar Dimples' and it makes him blush profusely. If they come into the room he tries to act like he's reading a magazine so he has something to hide behind. Especially if it's Brenda; she's this older lady that totally looks like a sweet grandma. When she learned of his nickname she actually walked up to him and pinched his cheeks. I laughed so hard I thought I was going to bust a stitch. It's pretty great and entertaining to see him bashful.

Tate studies me for a moment, unsure, "Doc, ahh, wants to talk to you about something by yourself, is that okay with you? I can stay if you're more comfortable." I give him a puzzled look. What on earth does the doctor need to talk to me about?

"No, stud, it's okay. I'll talk to Dr. Hopkins and then we can finally go home." Tate nods at us and walks out of my room, closing the door behind him.

"What's up, sir?"

"Well, may I sit, Emily?" He peers over at me, uneasily.

"Yes, sir, of course." Shit. Am I dying or something?

"Thanks." He takes a seat in the chair next to the bed. I sit up and scoot to the end of the bed, closer to him, in my pajamas decorated with Batman symbols. Tate thought they were hilarious, but we all know Batman is hot.

Dr. Hopkins continues, "You see, I wanted to talk to you not about the accident exactly, but about the person who ran into the vehicle you were in." He steeples his fingers under his chin as he says this and I notice a shiny silver watch on his wrist I've never seen before. Doctor Hopkins has good taste in watches. Shit what did he say? This medicine makes me a little loopy. *Focus, Emily.* Oh right, the idiot that hit us.

"You are aware that she is staying in this hospital as well? I believe Mr. Masterson already informed you, correct?"

"Yes, Tate told me about it when I first woke up."

"Right, that's good. Well, you see I was also her doctor because her injuries were so severe. This is all privileged information that I wouldn't normally ever give out. It's just that the circumstances are, well, they are just unlike anything I've dealt with in the past. Putting the legalities aside, I feel I have no choice but to share a few things with you."

"I have to be frank with you, Doc. You're kind of freaking me out right now."

"I assure you Emily, that is not what I'm attempting to do here. I'll share a little amount and we will go from there, okay?" I nod, uneasily.

"The patient, I had to restructure her left arm, wrist and left foot. I was shocked when I saw her and then saw you. So I took the liberty of comparing a few things. You see, I had to take your blood to run tests to make sure you could be on certain medications, check for unplanned pregnancies, your white cell count, etc. I had to take her blood samples for the same reason and also for the police to know her blood alcohol content." *Okay, and?*

I shoot Dr. Hopkins a 'so what' kind of look. "Okay, I'm aware of all that, I mean, did you need me to sign some more paperwork or something? Do you have liability sheets or something for blood work?"

"No, no, dear." He takes a deep breath and sets his hands down.

"You see, Emily, the person who hit you is Elaina Harper." He looks so sad to deliver this news, but I have no clue who this chick is. She has the same last name as I do, but what does that mean?

"I'm sorry but you will have to fill me in, Doc, because I have no idea who that is." He looks shocked to hear me say this and closes then opens his mouth again.

"You have no knowledge of her, whatsoever?"

"No sir, I would like to believe that I would remember her. I mean it is the same last name and all."

"Oh no. I wonder if even she knows." He shakes his head, his eyes with a faraway look in them.

After a moment he continues, "Emily, Elaina Harper is your identical twin. You don't know that you're a twin?"

I burst out laughing loudly, bending over and holding onto my stomach. The laughs turn to sobs and then I'm crying all over the place.

"You mean to tell me I have a sister, an identical twin sister, and she almost died because we were in a wreck together and she's right down the hall from me?" I gasp out in between sobs.

"Yes, that's exactly what I mean."

I rush to the bathroom as fast as I can and up-chuck my lunch of chicken and dumplings Mishka had made me, only called something different in Russian. *I can't believe I have a sister!* I thought all of my family was dead and the one person I have left in the world almost died. I have to see her. I have to meet her. I hear Tate enter the room and begin yelling at the doctor.

"What the hell's going on? Why is my Krasaaveetsa upset? I hope for your sake I don't have to hurt you, Doc."

Oh shit! I better go get Tate before he takes out the poor old doctor's knees. I open the door and step back into the room swiftly.

"Tate, relax sugar dimples. It's not the doctor's fault. He gave me some news and it made me upset, but he didn't do anything wrong." I glance to the doctor and see he looks like he's about to piss his pants. I don't blame him. Tate is a mean cookie when he goes all 'Mafia Boss.' Tate clears his throat and looks to the doctor.

"Sorry about that, Dr. Hopkins, just looking after my Krasaaveetsa. What is it? Wait, is she pregnant or something?" He gets a hopeful expression and it fills me full of warmth.

"Of course, Mr. Masterson, I understand. And no, sir, she is not pregnant. Miss Harper can fill you in on what she wishes to share."

Dr. Hopkins then meets my eyes, "Emily, she is in room 309 and you are on her list of allowed visitors. Good luck. I'll have your discharge paperwork drawn up and Nurse Brenda will be in here to have you sign everything."

"Okay, thank you, doctor." Tate steps to the side and Dr. Hopkins scuttles out of my room a little too eagerly.

"What is it, little pet? What happened?"

"Okay, first I need to get my clean clothes on. Then I need to go to room 309. Then I will tell you what's going on, but first I have to see it with my own eyes." I shuffle toward my bag of clothes Tate had London bring for me.

"What's in room 309? Oh, you mean the person who hit us? No, Krasaaveetsa, you stay out of there." Tate demands and crosses his arms like the decision's final.

Huffing, I argue, "No way, I'm not staying out of there!"

"The hell you aren't! I've already called Uncle Victor and he's going to take care of her. No one almost kills my Krasaaveetsa and then lives to talk about it. I don't know which it was, the Chinese or the Italians or maybe even those fucking bikers, but I will make this right. I'm so sorry you went through this." I pale at his words and want to puke again.

"HOLY FUCK, TATE!" I shriek spazzing out, "Call Victor back now! That's my twin sister in that room!"

I rip my clothes out of my bag, changing as quickly as possible. It's not that fast because my body hurts so badly still. Tate turns white as a ghost when he hears what I say about it being my sister and immediately dials his uncle.

"I'm sorry, Krasaaveetsa. Fuck! I had no clue. I didn't even know you had a sister. I'm so sorry, I will fix this."

"I didn't know about it either, it was kept secret from me I guess and I don't even know why. I swear to God, Tate, if something happens to her because of your Mafia shit, I will never forgive you." I grit, furious at him. I can't even look at him right now. He better fix this quick.

"I'm going to her room to see her."

"I wish you would wait, but if you insist, then I'm coming also so I can protect you if needed. I think I know who will be taking care of it, but just in case I'm wrong, I want to be there also."

"Protect me? Are you kidding right now? You calling hits on people that turn out to be my sister is NOT fucking protecting me!" I retort, storming out of my room and down the hall as fast as possible.

I notice his brother, Viktor, down the hall a little ways from me, about to enter into one of the hospital rooms off to the right side. What is he doing? It clicks all in place with Tate's family being mafia. *Oh God, please no!*

"Viktor!" I bellow and start walking quicker. He looks up at me, gives me a brief smile, and then goes into the room and closes the door.

I call out to Tate who's trailing behind me a few paces, "Oh my God, Tate! Please! Get Viktor!"

"Okay, baby." He takes off, sprinting the rest of the way. I attempt to catch up to them both, as quickly as my sore muscles will allow me too.

I burst into the room, door flying open and crashing into the wall. I end up right behind Tate, breathing deeply and freeze at what I see.

Viktor's standing at the end of my sister's bed, staring at her almost as if he's in a trance. His face is ashen as he catalogs Elaina's features. His fingertips tap the ends of each other, almost as if he has a rhythm thrumming through his mind.

"Viktor!" I gasp out and it finally makes him blink. He turns, twisting his head to be able to see me and squints, confused.

"N-no, p-please!" I plead desperately. I don't even know her, but I'm already willing to protect her. "Viktor, she's my sister. Tate didn't know any of that before he spoke to your uncle. Please, I beg you, don't hurt her." Viktor blinks and glances at my sister again. He nods and walks to her.

175

I attempt to run after Viktor, ready to jump on his back if I have to, but Tate is too quick and snatches my arm to stop me. I turn practically hissing at him and he covers my mouth, murmuring almost silently, to watch.

Viktor leisurely walks to Elaina's side and does the sign of the Russkaya Mafiya on her forehead. He gazes at her briefly and then bends down, tenderly applying a chaste kiss on the middle of her forehead.

"She's Krasaaveetsa too, da?" he questions Tate.

"Da, braat, she is a beauty like moy own Krasaaveetsa."

Viktor turns to me, taking in each of my facial features with a look of wonderment on his face, "There are two of you, printyessa?"

I gasp, nodding and the tears I've been holding, spill over my cheeks and trembling lips. "Yes, Viktor, there are two of me, but I didn't know that before. I just found out about her from the doctor."

I approach her side and peer down at her face; it looks exactly like mine. It's surreal to witness her lying there, motionless. Elaina's heavily medicated and sedated to help with the pain, so I doubt she will wake anytime soon. I wonder how she would feel about me. If she knows about me? Why was I left not knowing about her?

"Please don't hurt her, Viktor," I beg him again.

He glances at me remorsefully, "I promise Emily. I won't ever hurt her, I will keep her safe. You have my word."

I approach him, hugging him tightly. "Thank you, brother." I murmur into his jacket and he squeezes me tightly so I know he heard me.

Tate cuts in, taking my hand and tugging me to him easily. "Now, Krasaaveetsa, you can calm down again. We can go home so you can get some more rest and we can come back to visit her." He peers over my head at his brother, "Viktor, please call if she wakes or anything changes."

"I will, Luka. I will take care of her and speak to you both soon."

We say goodbye. I graze my sister's unmoving hand with mine, and then Tate and I head on our way to my room to get my stuff. Time to finally go home.

Sapphire Knight

Chapter 14

Tate

My God, I can't believe I almost had her sister, Elaina killed. I hope she forgives me. I can't lose her, I love her. We finally get past all the Jeremy bullshit and are now faced with yet another issue. I make another call to Uncle.

"Is my Krasaaveetsa sister still safe?"

"Da, but she should die for this."

"I don't care, Victor. Make sure everyone knows not to touch her."

"I will take care of it, nephew."

"Thank you."

"Da." He hangs up and I put my phone away.

Short and simple, just the way I like my calls to go.

Earlier, when I dropped Emily off at home, she was doing much better but was still a little upset. I really don't like her being distraught, so I'm hoping I can find out about Elaina for her. I'm going to call my boy, Hans, who works for my father and have him dig up whatever info on Elaina is possible. I'd like to get all of the secrets out into the open and not be blindsided again, literally and figuratively.

Thank fuck this semester is almost over with. I can't deal with classes and everything else. I need to be home more with my love. I have to talk to Emily about all of this and I'm not looking forward to the conversation. My poor girl has been through hell and back; the last thing I want to do is stress her out more so.

I arrive at my parents' house and one of the maids is already standing on the front porch. She's probably been standing there waiting to open the door for me since early this morning when I first called my father. He's a little obnoxious about stuff like that. Gizya is always treating people without consideration for their comfort.

I park my Mercedes on the circle drive and make my way up the grand front entryway that has four large, stone steps.

"Morning, Mr. Tatkiv," Marine murmurs politely.

"Morning Marine, how are you today?"

She opens the front door, following me in and murmuring, "I'm well, sir. Good day." She nods and quickly scuttles off to do whatever strenuous task my parents deemed necessary.

Gizya approaches, boasting a large smile.

"Atyets," I embrace my father and kiss his cheek out of respect.

I haven't always been close to my father. Growing up he was a hard man. Since Viktor and I have gotten older, we have both grown closer to our father. I think it's because we finally understand—at least partially—the stress and pressure he lives with, being The Big Boss here in America. When we lived in Russia he was always out on business. At least here he is able to be home more and is safe. I'm grateful I don't have to be the Big Boss. My father still has at least fifteen more years and then we will talk. I don't want my children growing up as I did.

"Sin." He has called me 'son' or 'Knees' my whole life and, in return, demanded I call him 'father' or 'Gizya'. Rarely have I been 'Luka' to him, unless I was being scolded or if we were surrounded by certain company.

"I came to ask for Mishka's ring."

I follow him to the bar right off the entry area. I have learned that my father is a busy man and it's best to get straight to the point. He appreciates it and it makes things easier. I take a seat on one of the black leather bar stools. Gizya rounds the bar, grabs up two chilled tumblers and tops them with a fresh bottle of Vodka.

"Ahh, I was surprised you didn't ask for it when you came for dinner. How is your little printyessa? Doing better, I hope."

I nod, taking a sip of my drink. "Emily is doing better. I just took her home before I came here. I'm assuming Viktor filled you in on the details with her sister?"

"Da, the little one hasn't woken up yet but Viktor seems quite taken with her."

"Oh, you picked up on that, too? I was wondering if I imagined it or not."

"I assure you, Viktor is thoroughly smitten. Uncle will have to pry Viktor's fingers from her, if anyone tries to get near her, let alone touch her. I am to assume you have Hans on her?"

"Da, I called Hans as soon as we left her room and I told him to find out anything he can about Elaina. Hans said to give him a few hours. I told him to call tomorrow because I plan to spend time with my Krasaaveetsa. I'm hoping she isn't too angry with me after my fuck up with the hit. Before this shit storm, she had agreed she would stay with me and let me have her forever. Then when we figured out whom Elaina is, Krasaaveetsa told me if anything happened to her saystraa (sister) that she would never forgive me. I want to give her Mishka's ring but I'm apprehensive that she will tell me no now."

"Ahh, moy sin, you have so much to learn about women yet. Emily will say yes, believe me. Do something special she will appreciate and show that you care about what she thinks is important. If you do, then she will come around." He takes a large swallow of his vodka.

"So, I should take care of her sister, Elaina? Move her to a suite? Maybe take my love her favorite ice cream? Or something extravagant, diamonds, a car she likes?" My father chuckles at how eager I am and my ideas.

"Da, move her sister so she's extra comfortable. You already have Viktor being your guard dog even though he was tasked with the actual hit in the first place. Take printyessa her favorite ice cream if that's something she

181

loves and slip Mishka's ring on her finger. Tell her you love her and she can pick out a new ring, if she doesn't want your grandmother's." I bite my lip, pondering over what my father suggests.

"Everything will work out, sin. Make sure to update Vivi and me. I know your mother is buzzing inside to plan a wedding. I am happy for you. You have our blessing and best wishes. We love you, Luka."

That's exactly what I needed to hear. Now, let's do this!

Emily

The next day...

I can't wait to meet my sister. *My sister.* Wow, that sounds so weird. I've always thought of London as my sister, but Elaina is actually the real deal. I'm filled with so much joy in my heart knowing I have a piece of family still alive in the world.

I shift in our bed and give Muffin a good scratch on his neck.

I glance back at Avery, as she chatters away, "I'm so glad you're back! We were all so worried about you. I brought you some hot chocolate back from A Sip of Heaven." Avery's planted beside me on the bed, "And I even brought you a banana nut muffin if London's fat ass hasn't eaten it already! I swear that girl has been eating everything in sight! I told her it was yours so she better leave it alone."

I lean over carefully and smooch her on her cheek. "Thank you, Avery, you are so thoughtful. With Mishka cooking for me the whole time I was in the hospital, I'm surprised I can fit in my own clothes!" Avery giggles at me and I grin. *It feels so good to be home.*

"Tate asked me to move in with him officially and he told me he loves me. It was the sweetest thing ever!"

She looks surprised but pleased and excited for me. "Wow, girl! That's so awesome, I'm happy for you! What are you going to do about your sister?" I had caught everyone up to speed when we arrived home yesterday.

"Umm, I just have to wait and see, I guess. It's so nerve racking." There's a small knock on the door and Muffin jumps up when it opens. In walks my gorgeous man carrying a small tub of my favorite ice cream—Cookies and Cream.

Avery's eyes go wide as she takes in the tub. "Yum, whatcha got there, stud?"

"Nothing for you," he chortles, teasing her. Avery huffs good naturedly, pretending to pout for a few seconds. It doesn't work so she gives me a small hug and stands up. Tate gives me a dazzling smile and walks toward the bed to set down the bag of stuff he has on the side table.

"I'll give you guys some privacy, love ya, Em! Holler if you need me, 'k?" Avery heads toward the door to leave and on the way she smacks Tate, dead center on the ass. He gawks at me as if he was just violated and I burst out in giggles. Avery smirks mischievously and winks, before she closes the door.

After the door shuts, I lean over and see that Tate has brought me a soda and ice cream. They are my two favorite guilty pleasures.

"Yum. Somebody's being sweet tonight!" I mumble as he bends down to lay next to me and gives me a chaste kiss on my forehead.

"Of course, my love. I want you happy and feeling better."

"I do feel much better. I think I just needed to be home and able to snuggle with Muffin."

"Good, Krasaaveetsa, that makes me happy." Tate huffs, "Muffin is not supposed to be on the bed."

I just shrug, 'cause the dog's on the bed and he's not going anywhere.

"I had your sister moved to a suite at the hospital and Viktor is staying with her."

I lean over and pull him to me so I can kiss him properly. "Thank you honey bun. That means more to me than you could ever imagine," I whisper, then slip my tongue between his lips and get a small kiss out of him. He pulls away and I suck on his bottom lip. God, I missed being so close to him.

Tate clears his throat. "Another thing, my Krasaaveetsa, is that I love you and I meant what I said earlier."

He takes my hand, drawing it in front of him to rest on his thigh. I watch, curious what his plans are and I'm thoroughly surprised when he pulls something out of his pocket. Tate covers my hand with both of his, as he sneakily slides a beautiful diamond ring on my finger.

I jerk my hand back to look closely at what he just put on me. I shoot my hand out in front of us, spreading my fingers wide; peering at the ring and see it's a large, round diamond. I'm guessing four carats with a wide platinum band. It's absolutely breathtaking and compliments my petite hand perfectly. People could see it fifty feet away, advertising that I'm taken, that I belong to someone, and that I'm loved.

It's so perfect it brings tears to my eyes. I look up at Tate in wonderment. I can't believe I have this great man in my life.

"Oh, Tate!" I choke, ready to start blubbering like an excited mess.

"It was Mishka's before, but if you don't like it, we can get you whatever ring you want. As long as it's my ring on your finger, I don't care what it looks like," he seriously declares, and I chuckle with a shaky smile.

"My God! This was Mishka's ring? It's even more perfect, I'm so honored to wear your grandmother's ring! Thank you, Tate, it's absolutely wonderful. I love you so much!" His smile beams brightly at my reaction and I can tell it pleases him that I love his grandmother's ring so much.

"I love you so much, Krasaaveetsa, truly," he murmurs, peppering soft kisses all over my face. "You make me so happy, Emily. Vivi is going to go through the roof with excitement when she hears that she will get the wedding she wants so badly to happen. I know she will want to help you plan all of it. Of course it will be whatever you want but she will be thrilled to just be a part of it. Mishka, too, if you don't mind their help?"

"No, of course not! I would love their help, but not too soon, okay?" Tate looks at me perplexed like he doesn't understand.

"I can wait six months, Krasaaveetsa, anything later and I will take you to Vegas to elope." I laugh at his time limit. He shoots me a look like he just solved world hunger.

"I guess I can try to pull it off in six months! But, I'm not giving up school."

"No, baby, you do whatever makes you happy. You want to go to school, go. You want to open a business, I will buy you one. You want to stay home and have my babies, let's do it. I want you to be as happy as I am, little lamb." *Oh, he's so freaking sweet!*

I think I've patiently waited long enough. I start to peel his clothes off of him and push him to lean backward. The pain meds the doctor gave me are freaking awesome. They make me feel pretty good, considering how badly my body hurt when I first woke up after the accident. I finish undressing Tate. Once he's naked and lying on the bed, I pause to take him in for a minute. God, he's fucking gorgeous. I want him so badly.

"Okay, big boy, we are gonna put this yummy ice cream to use." He gazes at me with wide eyes and a sexy little smirk.

I grab up the ice cream tub and spoon from the small, wooden side table. Smearing a little melted ice cream across the ridges of his abs, I bend, lapping and sucking up each drop. I make my way up and down, savoring over each firm, ice cream covered crest on his washboard stomach.

Placing a small spoonful of deliciousness on each nipple, I smear it in cold circles with the spoon. I continue licking over his barbells, then draw them each into my mouth, sucking strongly.

"Mm," Tate groans at the cool sensations and then the heat from my mouth. Moving up, I bite his neck and he growls deeper, pushing my hips down, closer to his cock. I know he wants me to grind down onto him. So I stall, peppering kisses down his tummy. I eventually make my way down to his engorged cock.

I take his dick in my hand, squeezing slightly and then pump him a few times. I give Tate a mischievous smile and take a bite of ice cream. Quickly, I lean in and take his cock in my mouth. I swirl the ice cream over his tip with my tongue and he groans. *Good, he must like it.* I slurp all the ice cream off him which he seems to like the most, moaning and gripping the sheet tightly attempting not to hurt me with my injuries. I bob my head up and down his length a few times, attempting to take him in as deeply as possible. He pulls me up quickly by my shoulders and his dick comes out with a loud pop.

"Poshyol (fuck), baby! Jesus, you are going to make me come already, that is fucking amazing." He tugs me up to him closer, turning, so he can lay me on my back.

He carefully takes off my night shirt, bra and thong, staring at me the entire time like he's a starved man.

He climbs between my legs and I protest, "No, Tate, I want to ride you!"

"Nuh uh. It's my turn, Emily." Tate scoots down and grabs a big bite of ice cream. He zeros in, going straight for my clit, it's a shocking zing of cold and then a shot of warm relief once the ice cream is gone.

"Fuck, Tate!" I cry loudly.

Tate takes another bite of ice cream then goes back down. He licks through my pussy lips, lapping at them as if he can't get enough. His tongue is shockingly cold from the ice cream. *God, it feels fantastic.* He sinks a warm finger deep inside me, and I'm so close I almost shoot off.

He stops eating my pussy to suck each of my nipples into his mouth, they pop out of his mouth and he lightly twists and tugs on them with his fingers. "God, you are so fucking sexy with my ring on your finger, Emily. To know this pussy is all mine, I can eat it and fuck it whenever I want to, turns me on so fucking much. My pussy, baby, mine," he murmurs, breathily.

"Oh, Tate, it feels so good." My body is writhing against his and my pussy is soaked, wanting him inside of me.

Tate kisses up to my neck aligning his cock at the one place I want him the most. He bites my shoulder harshly, causing me to let loose a loud scream while he thrusts deep inside of me quickly. He pumps hard once, seating himself in me to the hilt and I start to come. Tate has me so worked up I can't think of anything but how good he feels, he glides in and out of me easily, the gush of wetness aiding him as my pussy convulses.

He pulls my legs up over his shoulders. "Ahhh!" I cry out, sore from the wreck but in too much pleasure to tell him to stop.

Tate's right hand grabs onto the headboard. I hear the bed creak and groan as he drives into me hard and rough. It's like he's making sure that tomorrow everyone will know where he has been. Raking my nails into his back, I suck one of his nipples into my mouth, nibbling each time he pulls away to drive into me again.

I know my body will hurt afterwards, but I can't bring myself to care through the pleasurable haze he has caused. My pussy contracts around his cock, pulling him in and it's his undoing. I feel his large cock jerk within me as his cum spurts deep inside. Each throb feels fantastic, sending shocks of pleasure through me.

Tate keeps his dick seated inside of me for a few minutes, resting and breathing deeply, until he is able to catch his breath. He rains kisses all over my face again. It's easily becoming one of my favorite things he does.

Tate mumbles, "Fucking amazing, Krasaaveetsa. I'm going to keep my cock here, so my cum stays deep inside of you. God, I fucking love you."

I grin up at him; he's sweaty and his hair is sticking out in every direction. The pleased look compliments his features very well. His magnificent body shines from the light coat of sweat glistening on his skin. I'm surrounded by the crisp scent from his body wash and it makes me feel safe and loved.

I'm finally home.

"I love you, too, sugar dimples. Now, let's hop in the shower, okay?" He nods and stands up from the bed.

Tate reaches down to pick me up tenderly and carries me bridal style to the bathroom. He turns on the massive garden tub and lets the water heat up, before he helps me into it with him. In the bath, he washes my body softly and gently massages my sore muscles, relaxing me all over.

I have never felt so cherished in my entire life. After our relaxing bath, we snuggle in our huge bed and he takes me lovingly, making sweet love to me two more times that night.

Chapter 15

Emily

Viktor calls us first thing in the morning to inform us that Elaina is finally awake and to share the conversation they had already. Apparently, Elaina asked who he was and Viktor told her that he was a friend, asking her if she had family. He played it off like he was going to call them for her but Elaina told him no, that she was adopted and doesn't communicate with her adopted family.

Viktor asked her why she was drinking and driving so irresponsibly and Elaina just told him she has a shitty life, which she didn't want to share any of it with him. He asked if she had a sister and Elaina told him not that she knows of, but her biological family never contacted her growing up. He informed Tate she seems sincere and he believes her.

Tate, of course, had Viktor on speaker phone, so I heard the entire conversation. I can't believe she has no idea of me either. Viktor said it took him a while to get her to stop weeping after he asked her about the drinking and driving. He thinks she was genuinely sorry and horrified that she almost killed Tate and me. Personally, I really have no idea what to think about any of this with her.

Shortly after the phone conversation with Viktor, one of his men—a guy named Hans—called to let him know what all information he found on Elaina. Hans basically confirmed what Viktor said about her. According to him, Elaina is twenty years old, born on August twenty-third (same as me), works at a shitty little bar in Knoxville called Root's, drives a white 2010 Chevrolet Camaro (good choice), lives in a shitty dump of an apartment, was adopted, no prior run-ins with the law, and has no boyfriend.

Hmm. I'm dying inside to go and see her. I wonder if she would share more about herself with me, if she knew I was her sister. I wonder if it will freak her out seeing that we look exactly alike. It sure as fuck tripped me out.

I huff, irritated over this breakfast dish sitting in front of me. I have way too much going on to worry about food right now. I appreciate Tate going out of his way to make it for me, and I'm sure it's absolutely delicious, but I'm just not in the mood.

"We will go, Krasaaveetsa, as soon as you eat your food so you can take your pain meds," Tate chastises me, with his eyebrow raised. I can't help it if I'm excited and it's making me not hungry!

"Tate, you have been on me for like twenty minutes buddy. I'm not freaking hungry! I will take some Tylenol, but not the strong stuff, okay? I'm feeling a lot better and I don't want to be loopy at the hospital." I send him my puppy dog face and puff out my bottom lip. He'll give in, he loves me too much.

Groaning, he rubs the back of his neck. "Alright, Krasaaveetsa, but if you start to get weak then you eat what I get for you, okay?" I grin triumphantly and nod. *I win.*

We finish getting dressed, me extra hurriedly attempting to rush Tate. He doesn't even need anything but a T-shirt and pants but he insists on hair gel, body spray, et cetera. Once I'm finally able to shuffle him out the door, he steers me to the Tahoe.

We load up, heading in the direction of the hospital. Tate's been a little paranoid driving me, so he's been driving the big ass Tahoe everywhere. I feel like we could crunch over cars with his SUV if we wanted to.

"Hey, sugar dimples; you think the Tahoe would make it over that little Honda?" I point at a silver Honda Civic, as it slowly passes us. He glances over at me as if I've lost my mind. I nod toward the car in question and then I shrug.

"What? It's a good question since we *are* in a monster truck."

"Oh my God, Emily, you are so annoying when you get hyped up. We are not in a monster truck; she's only got a three-inch lift and thirty-five inch tires. It just feels huge to you because you are bite size." He shakes his head and goes back to paying attention to the road.

"Are you sure personality disorders don't run in your family?"

"Stop, Emily. Just shut your mouth before you get me wound up." I roll my eyes at him.

"Okay, fine, I was just asking. I mean you did just get pissy again."

"Shh."

"Oh my God! Did you just shush me? You freaking, shh!" He just rolls his eyes and ignores me. I feel kind of bad for him after a moment, but I can't help it. I'm so nervous I feel like I could blow chunks everywhere.

We arrive at the hospital and I'm still all jittery. Tate is annoyed because apparently I "bounce around and shit." I do kind of feel like I'm bouncing when I walk, but I won't openly admit that to him.

Tate and I walk through the hospital up to Dr. Hopkins wing with the private suites and finally arrive. I breathe deeply, taking in the large number '5' on the door.

Suite 5

Tate raps lightly on the closed door. I can hear Viktor through the thin metal, shuffle around and inform Elaina that he has a surprise visitor for her. After a moment, Viktor opens the door and he looks...happy, like really happy. Tate and I smile at him and he smiles back. He even shows teeth in his smile. Well, I'll be damned, either he has a crush or she's just a really cool chick.

Viktor shuffles over so we can step inside. I gradually make my way around the entry and the corner in the suite, full of nerves.

Elaina's propped up in bed with a few pillows and is looking bruised up, but remarkably better. I check her over completely, taking note of every detail. Eventually, I meet her eyes that look exactly like mine, except where mine are a light green hers are a really deep, sapphire blue.

She looks me over as thoroughly as I had done with her and when she finally takes in my face, she lets loose a blood curdling scream.

I drop to the floor, frightened after everything I've been through and cover my head with my arms. Tate turns around swiftly to see who's behind me and Viktor rushes to pull her to his chest.

Elaina stops screaming and starts to stutter, "Vi-vi-vi-Viktor who-who the fuck was that? Oh m-my God, Viktor, she looked exactly like me!"

I can hear her start to cry and it makes me sad inside. I know on the pain killers it has to make things probably even weirder for her, as they did for me. Tate spins back around and realizes the reason Elaina screamed is because of me. Viktor is clutching her to his chest, his arms covering the side of her face so they are in their own little cocoon of safety. He's mumbling something to her that I can't hear.

Tate leans down to help me up, worried. "Are you okay, Krasaaveetsa?" I nod and stand up with his help.

I hear Elaina question Viktor if my name is Krasaaveetsa and it makes me giggle. She peaks her head around Viktor when she hears me, reminding me of a curious child.

"I'm fine, Tate, she just startled me." I pat my shirt and glance at him. "With everything that's been going on, I figured the best move was to hit the floor." I peer over at her and offer her a shy smile. Elaina returns my little smile but also looks weary.

I should say something.

"Umm, hi, Elaina. You ran into me with your car." *Shit.* I wince, did I really just open up with that? Fuck, I have to think before I speak!

"I did?" She chews her fingernail, nervously. "I'm so, terribly sorry if you are hurt because of me." Her voice is softer than mine and I just want to hug her.

"Can I come closer so we can talk, please?" I request quietly, I don't want to freak her out again.

"Yes, of course you can."

I smile and sit on the edge of her bed. "So I'm guessing by your reaction, you are just as shocked about this as I am?"

Elaina sighs, nodding. "Completely, I had no idea I had any biological family close to me or any family at all, for that matter." That really sucks but it makes me feel better that this is a big surprise to her as well.

I can't help but feel that I got cheated as I gaze at her. I could have known her. I could have grown up with her, shared things with her, loved her. I could have had my very own sister.

"Well, I'm actually from Texas. I grew up there my whole life. I just moved here a few months ago; I go to the college at UT. And technically I'm the only biological family left. Everyone else has passed away," I finish, mumbling. *Calm down.* I'm rambling.

She chuckles sadly, "And what are the odds that on my very shitty night, I get smashed drunk and wreck into my identical twin? The twin that I've never personally met or even knew anything about, for that matter? That's really creepy if you think about it. I'm such a fuck up. I don't know how to make this better." Wow, she rambles too.

"Yep, very creepy, but it must have happened for a reason."

"We have a lot to talk about."

I nod, "Definitely."

I give her a kind smile, lifting her hand in mine and giving it a light squeeze. Elaina returns my smile and it's like looking into a mirror. Such a surreal feeling.

We spend the next two hours comparing our likes and dislikes. It's amazing how much we have in common with us never even knowing about the other one. She's like me, getting excited and gesturing with her hands while she talks. Or does that make it me gesturing like her? Viktor seems relaxed and in good spirits. Tate and he speak but not very much, he mostly just sits, watching Elaina like he's oblivious to everything else in the world.

Tate and I take our leave but exchange phone numbers prior, promising to call if we thought of something new we were curious about. I also swore to her that I will be back at dinnertime and bring her some homemade soup. Elaina has to stay in the hospital for a while for her body to heal. During that time I'm going to get to know my sister.

Three weeks later...

It's been three weeks since I first met my sister and I love her to pieces. It's like I've found a clone, discovering all the things she does, eats, likes, et cetera. She's pretty much become an instant best friend. We've even introduced her to all of our other friends.

London and Avery seem a little on edge, unsure about her, but I know they will come around the more they get to know her. They've actually been hanging out more with each other, since I've been spending so much time getting to know Elaina. I knew those two would become good friends though; they are more alike than they realize. Ever since that first day, London showed up in the courtyard at the college and they trumped my vote to go out.

Elaina ended up losing her job from that shithole bar, Roots. Tate gave her a new, better paying job at OO7. According to Tate, Viktor prefers 007 to Tainted so he told Tate to let her work at 007, because he has to be able to keep an eye on her.

I personally think it's way too soon for her to be working and so does Dr. Hopkins. She barely got released two days ago. Elaina was stubborn and declared that she would lose her apartment if she didn't go to work, and refused any of Viktor's help.

She enlightened me that for the past week, Viktor was trying to get her to stay with him at his house. I think it's a great idea since it's a lot closer to Tate's house and I can see her more, but that's not my business. If Viktor is at all as persistent as Tate, Elaina won't stand a chance fighting against him. With some of the shit she told me she's been through, though, she definitely deserves a little piece of happiness.

It's a Friday night and London called earlier, wanting us to all go out. I'm feeling way better, almost completely healed up. Most of the cuts that I received from the accident that will leave marks will disappear in a few years, since they weren't too deep. I still have a few marks from the deeper bruises left but they have faded so much, that they are barely visible. After Dr. Hopkins ran all the tests, he informed me that I have something that causes me to bruise more than average and stay bruised up longer. I can't remember what he called it, but it sucks.

My body has looked like I was beaten up for weeks now. I'm sick of people glaring at Tate when we go shopping or to eat. They have no idea just how much of a good man he truly is.

London and Cameron are still up and down since I got into the wreck. I can't believe they've even lasted this long. London must really care for him. Normally, she would have kicked him to the curb by now. She's too smart for her own good, though; she ends up getting bored easily.

Avery and Nikoli still date occasionally but are not serious. I guess they're both satisfied with their friends with benefits situation and I'm happy for them both. I think they're both lonely and will end up moving forward when someone new comes into the picture. I don't know though, I could be wrong.

Viktor and my sister are adorable. Viktor is constantly chasing her and trying to woo her. I kind of hope she eventually gives him a chance; I think he could make her really happy.

I peek out of the kitchen looking for Tate.

"Honey bun!" I holler for Tate.

I think he's in the living room watching ESPN. I was so happy to find out he likes sports because I love football and baseball. I don't like to watch a lot of games but if one's on, then I will certainly take the time and check it out.

"Yeah, Krasaaveetsa?" he bellows back. I was right. I find him in the living room with ESPN muted and texting on his phone.

"Hey, stud, London texted me and asked if we all wanted to go to OO7 tonight. I know my sister's off and Avery already said she wants to go, too. Are you up for it or should I just plan a girl's night out?"

He grabs my arm and tugs me onto his lap. I love being on his lap, it's so comfy. "Yes, little lamb, we will go. Is Cam going, do you know? I'll text Viktor and Niko, I'm sure they will want to tag along."

"I don't know about Cameron," I shrug, "but I would think so if London's going."

"Okay, cool, baby. Text London back and I'll text the guys." He smooches me on the lips and pats my thigh so he can stand up. Knowing Tate he's going to go scour his closet for something to wear. That man is as bad as a female when it comes to what he's going to wear somewhere.

I head back to the kitchen for my phone and excitedly text London back.

Me – Yep we're in! Did you ask my sister too?

L – Of course I did! 9:30 p.m.?

Me – It's a date!

L – Sounds good.

Me – Yaay!

I finish with texting London and instantly pull up Elaina's number.

Me – Hey beautiful sister, do you want a ride and a place to crash tonight since we're going out?

We didn't file any charges against her. Tate wanted to, but I refused to on my part and he followed suit. Elaina still got her license suspended for a while, since she was a dumbass and drove while drinking. The judge let up some, but not completely. Thank God for Tate's connections or it probably would have been a lot worse for her.

E – No thanks Viktor just texted me and said he was on his way.

Me – Already? London told me 9:30

E – Yes he wants to have dinner first.

Me – OOOHHHHH!!! Have fun. I'll see you soon!

E – I will. Smooches. Favorite sister, ever.

Me – Ever, Ever!

I close out of Elaina's message box, with a large smile on my face. Pulling up Avery, I'm confident I already know her answer.

Me – Hey babe, you want a ride and a place to sleep after the club tonight?

A – You know this! I'll be over to your casa about 9ish?

Me – Awesomesauce!

A – Just like me!

Me – Lmao yep!

I turn the screen off, slipping the phone into my pocket. Now that I have everything as far as rides and who all is going taken care of, it's time for me to get dressed. That's always the hardest part for me. I strive to find a balance of sexy and classy.

I skip to the bedroom, excited to finally see all of my friends at once, since it's been awhile. Sure enough, Mr. GQ himself is going through his closet like a mad man. My own closet has grown considerably in size as well.

I think Tate has a shopping addiction. To him it's all normal because he grew up like this. I grew up shopping at Walmart and looking for sales. Huge difference. Once he found out the sizes of my clothes and shoes, random shit just started to show up at the house all of the time.

It all started with Victoria's Secret because he knows I love their stuff. That changed, growing into shoes and now, it has progressively gotten to him buying absolutely everything. He blames it on me, saying I don't have enough stuff, while I tell him he has too much.

I'm not really upset though, I love having him spoil me. I try to give him a hard time about it, but also make sure he knows I'm grateful. Today's delivery consisted of a silver bracelet and matching necklace, both with my initial on them, which I love! In fact I'm going to wear my new bracelet tonight.

Tate decides on a pair of dark wash regular/relaxed jeans that make his ass look fantastic. His ass is juicy enough in his boxer briefs; I always tease him that I could bounce a quarter off it. He pairs them with a white button-down shirt and rolls the sleeves up. Yum, he looks fantastic.

If he's going to be that spiffy, then I'm going to hussy it up and wear a new dress he bought me. It's a tight, short, red dress with a red lace overlay. I pick out a sexy, red lace G-string and a red lace push-up bra. Gotta help the girls out as much as possible and these push-up bras are perfect to give a little cleavage.

I snatch up a pair of leopard print heels. They have red bottoms on them that nicely match my dress. Tate said they would look sexy on me when the box showed up last week and I have to agree with him.

I slip the gorgeous shoes on to test out my walk. I get a little wobbly if they're too high. I walk from one end of the closet and back. They don't feel bad actually. Man, whatever these shoes are, they are freaking comfy for having such high heels on them.

Satisfied with my outfit, I fix my makeup in a smoky eye, black mascara and nude lipstick. There, all set and ready.

I make my way to the living room catching little whiffs of Tate's cologne. He's wearing the cologne that I love so much—Hugo Boss. I feel like I could walk behind him and just sniff him all day.

The doorbell chimes and Muffin starts barking excitedly. Awesome, that should be Avery.

As I walk to the front door, I pass the hall leading to Cameron's door and hear loud, obnoxious female moans. *Well, fuck!* That's definitely not London in there. That asshole is going to break her heart and I'm going to end up being evil for having to tell her about it. I don't know what on earth he could be thinking right now, especially doing it here where everyone will notice.

Tate, Avery, Niko and I all ride in the Tahoe to the club. Much safer to all go together and have a designated driver. Plus I love having Tate and Niko when we go out, it makes me feel safe. Tate's not huge, but he's very strong, and Nikoli, well he's huge.

We arrive at OO7, get settled in and I have to admit it's way different tonight, than it was the first night we came. I love the fact that Tate owns the club. I never noticed it before, but we get treated extra well because Tate's the Boss. If we want to hear a certain song it magically gets played pretty quickly after we request that we want to hear it.

One thing I have learned about my twin is that we are opposites, when it comes to partying. I prefer to dance but I rarely drink. I can have a good time without having alcohol.

Elaina though, is the crazy one. I thought London was bad! London likes to get sloshed and take off with guys she meets or whatever. Elaina is the type where her ass is dancing on top of the bar and doing body shots. Tate takes it all in stride. He's obviously used to the party scene since he owns two clubs. Viktor, however, watches Elaina like a hawk. I think he wishes he would have become a Boss now.

Avery and Niko dance together and have fun. At least one set of our friends know how to co-exist easily.

Cameron is a no show right now, but I'm sure that's for the best. He's probably busy getting rid of his secret booty call from the house. I talked to Tate about it and I'm still not sure what to really do about it just yet.

Tate scoots closer to me in the VIP booth and kisses the tip of my nose, causing me to blink. "You doing okay, baby?" He murmurs next to my ear, so I can hear him over the thumping music.

I nod, grinning at him and drinking my water.

Avery approaches the table with Niko, huffing from dancing for a few songs, "No one else is here yet?" she questions, loudly.

"Nope, nobody except us and my sister!"

"That sucks!" Avery replies and downs her martini.

I glance over toward the entrance and London finally comes through the door. She's all dolled up, looking like the old London, before she came to Tennessee and got used to T-shirts and boxer shorts. She's got on a black 'pin-up girl' style dress, that's covered with little red cherries. London has her long, black hair down, her face all painted up with her red lipstick and she's in some sky high red shoes. She looks so freaking hot!

I stand up and wave at her, so she knows where we are. I see someone come up behind her, but can't make him out. She's already tall, throw on some really high shoes and she towers over a lot of people. The guy puts his arms through her arms, from behind her, resting them against her stomach, as they walk leisurely.

Oh My God, I'm going to kill Cameron! She reaches down and threads her fingers through his, leading him to the VIP section.

They make it to the top of the stairs and I about fall out of the booth.

"Holy shit," I murmur, but no one hears me.

That's definitely not Cameron Wentworth! Hell no, she went to the extreme opposite. This man has a short, trimmed, black beard, black hair in a faux hawk and light grey eyes. He's probably six foot and built muscular, like a brawler. He's covered in tattoos from his neck down to his fingers.

My mouth waters as I check him over. She did damn good this time. The new guy is wearing faded, loose fit jeans, black motorcycle boots and a plain black T-shirt. Sweet Jesus, I feel like I need to high-five London right now. This new guy fits her pin-up self, like they were made for each other.

She makes it to the table, standing in front of us, smiling widely. "Hey guys, this is Cain. Cain, this is everybody!" London yells and he laughs, gazing at her like she's the best thing he's ever seen.

"Hi, Cain, nice to meet you." I do a little wave like a dork, greeting him with a friendly smile and Tate just nods at him. Ah, he's definitely in The Boss mode.

"'Sup." He nods at us both, and goes quiet.

They get settled in the booth, with Cain sitting on the outside, and London next to me, while Avery and Niko dance some more.

Tate looks away and I give London a thumbs-up and a huge smile, "Jackpot, friend!" I nod towards the hottie sitting next to her.

"Fucking right!" she hollers back and grins.

Well, looks like London's back to her normal self. Everything's going great, we're having fun at the table, screaming out the lyrics to 'American Woman' by Lenny Kravitz and generally just being silly. None of us are really drinking, I think we all just wanted to be out and about. Elaina has been doing body shots from the bar and Viktor has been silently watching the entire time, fuming.

London pulls my attention away from my sister, "So, I have a secret! Well it's not mine, it's Cain's."

"Okay, what is it?" I ask bluntly, she knows I am too nosey.

"Cain is a nickname! Do you remember a boy we went to school with named Brandon Meeks?" London leans over and whispers loudly in my ear.

"Yeah, of course! Didn't he like move in sixth or seventh grade or something?" Where's she going with this?

"Yes, exactly! That's who Cain is! He and a bunch of his friends rode into town for a few days to take care of a couple things."

"Wait, they rode in on motorcycles?"

"Yes!" She beams, excitedly. "Isn't it awesome? I have so much to tell you, this isn't the first time Cain and I have seen each other. We actually started talking again before I came out here, when I was still in Texas. I'll fill you in on everything when we have a minute and it's not so loud, okay?" She looks at me excitedly.

"Okay, sounds good!" Sounds like she has a lot she needs to tell me, besides this mess with Cameron. Since when did London stop talking to me about everything? I don't know whether to be upset or sad. I know I've been really busy spending time with Elaina and Tate, but I need to talk to her more. She's my best friend and I'm not being a very good friend to her, if I don't know what's going on. I am happy to see she's not moping around over Cam, though. London spilled a drink, so Cain headed over to the bar with her for something to clean it up with.

Well speaking of, Cameron treks up the stairs to the VIP and gazes around, looking straight for London. When he finally spots her, he looks murderous. I had told Tate about what I heard from Cameron's door and that things might get awkward between him and London.

I elbow Tate enough to get his attention, "Sugar Dimples, Cam just showed up and he looks pissed. You might have an altercation if you don't go and get him."

I point over towards Cameron and Tate's beautiful hazel eyes narrow to find Cameron storming toward London and her new beau. *Oh man.* Cain looks like he will rip Cameron apart if shit gets started. Why can't we just have one night where we can all be together and not have some kind of drama?

Tate jumps up, quickly making his way to Cameron. He intercepts Cam before he can end up getting too close to London. Cain watches everything, perked up, looking like he's ready to mop the floor with Cameron, if needed.

Elaina flops down in the booth next to me, huffing, irritated, "I just heard Viktor's freaking going around telling any guys that want to approach me, that I'm his! Can you believe this asshole?" I look at my sister and burst out laughing. She has no idea what she's into.

"Oh God, Elaina, just give in. If he's going around and claiming you to other men then you're as good as his. Trust me on this; I have already fought this battle with Tate. Viktor will drive you absolutely mad until you realize that you love the idiot too much, to let him go." If Viktor wants her, he's bound to get her eventually.

Konstantin would go nuts if both of his sons were to settle down and embrace the Russian Mafia as much as he wants them to. Tate has discussed with me that he has been moving more and more toward Mafia business only. He said it's important since it will affect my life as well. I'm not worried though, I know my man will make a great Big Boss if it comes to that.

Elaina rolls her eyes, arguing, "Whatever, he can try all he wants, but it's not happening." I just smile and nod, yes, my dear sister, it looks like it will happen.

She has no clue that this is exactly how the Ginzburg men work. They see what they want and go after it until it's theirs. Tate's momma, Vivi, told me all about Konstantin chasing her back in the day. I guess their marriage was more of an arrangement, but according to her she didn't make it easy for him at all.

I gaze over toward Tate, Cameron is yelling and gesturing with his hands. London's just smiling at Cain and acting like Cam doesn't exist. I know inside she loves it that he's so furious! After a few beats, Tate wraps his arm around Cameron's shoulders, trying to calm him down.

My sister gets torn up off a few more shots she does and Viktor has to practically carry her out of the club. He chastises her but you can see he enjoys getting the chance to take care of her. I offer to let her come home with us but he isn't letting anyone near her. I think it's adorable. I know Viktor will take good care of her and make her life easier. After seeing how hard she works and how little she has, she deserves her life to be a little easier and happier. I don't know everything but we have talked a lot about how different each of our lives were growing up, and hers was very hard. I wish I would have had the chance to have her by my side growing up. I think my life would have turned out a lot differently, as would hers. She doesn't know it yet but Tate's giving her time off so she can come with the family to Russia for Christmas. I guess Viktor had asked Tate before I even had a chance to.

Tate finally gets Cameron to leave and we all decide it's time to head home. This night was awesome, besides the altercation with London and Cam. I got to relax with the girls and my man, what's better than that?

Chapter 16

Emily

Four months later- March 27th...

I stare blankly at myself in the wide mirror. We have the opulent Presidential suite for three blissful nights. The magnificent room is in the same hotel that has the large ballroom we rented for the wedding. I can't believe today is my wedding day. I know it was fast, but at the same time it feels as if I've been waiting forever to marry the love of my life. I blink, feeling my eyes starting to crest with tears.

London huffs, griping at me, "Girl, don't you dare cry and mess up your face. You look beautiful but I can't fix red rimmed eyes! Plus you don't want mascara dripping on that enormous dress of yours."

I gaze at my reflection once more, taking in the beautiful hand stitching and lace on my dress. This dress was designed specifically for me. I told the designers what I wanted, they drew it up and then they made it.

Tate's mother Vivi, and grandmother, Mishka, took me dress shopping. It was the worst and best experience ever, all rolled into one. I have never tried on so many dresses in my entire life. It got to the point where eventually the boutique called in a well-known designer to just make what it was that I wanted. I was exhausted but also extremely happy. My mother and grandmother are in Heaven, or I know they would have been the ones helping me, so to have family there to support me and be a part of it all, was beyond a great experience.

I sniffle, "I can't help it, London! Everything's just so perfect. I'm so blessed to have you guys in my life, marrying the man of my dreams, I have family here to stand beside me, all these changes and I'm just so fortunate my life turned out like this." A tear leaks out of my left eye and I try to hide it.

Avery walks back into the dressing area, glances at me and shakes her head, scolding me, "Geez! Is she crying again? When will you stop, woman? Today's a good day. Be happy and quit your damn crying, you're an emotional mess today, Emily!"

"I know," I clear my throat, "I know it, I'm just so lucky and extremely happy." A few more tears trickle out and both of them roll their eyes at me. *Bitches!*

London hugs Avery and grins at me, "Thank you, I was just telling her that!"

Elaina pops in the room, "Hey, hookers, leave my sweet, little sister alone!"

This shit again. Elaina's been teasing me for the past few months that she's older but I know I have to be the older one. She won't show me her birth certificate so I know she's fibbing.

"Ah! You, are the little sister. Clearly I'm bigger." She starts to laugh evilly.

"Yes, you are definitely bigger in the waist!" I start to throw everything that is surrounding me and she takes off running.

"I'm taking back all of your key cards!" I threaten and they all laugh at me.

"She's going to cry again, dammit!" London yells at my sister.

Elaina holds her hand out for me to grab, "Come on, cry baby, it's time for you to go officially belong to that hunk standing at the altar."

I can't believe London even had the energy to fix me all up like this and touch it up a few times too, since I keep crying. I shoot her a wobbly smile, full of gratitude and she smirks at me, with a teasing glint in her eyes.

I breathe deeply and let it out in a whoosh, "Okay, you girls go stand up there and keep my spot for me."

Avery starts giggling at me and hugs me, "You dork, Tate would shoot their asses if they tried to take your spot!"

I shrug, "Eh, wouldn't be the first time he shot someone for me." I wink and smile.

She probably thinks I'm being silly and fibbing. Very few people know what all Tate has done for me. I do and I'm grateful my fiancé likes to keep me safe, and by any means necessary.

The girls go ahead of me to take their places in the ballroom. Konstantin, Tate's father is patiently waiting for me in the hallway when I open the suite's large, mahogany door. He smiles widely, his face lighting up when he sees me.

"Ahhh! Little printyessa, such Krasaaveetsa! You look like a true printyessa in the big, fluffy dress!" Konstantin opens his arms wide, embracing me in a warm hug and sweetly kisses me on my cheek. He came to walk me down the aisle and give me away to Tate. I've gotten close to Tate's parents, which they love. I'm over the moon happy that he asked if it was okay for him to walk me down the aisle. I was thinking about asking Elliot to come and do it, but this way is better.

I beam a bright smile, "Yes, thanks to Vivi and Mishka! They did such a wonderful job with planning the wedding. I would have been lost without them." I loop my arm through his, grasping on his elbow as he leads me down the hallway to my beloved.

I chatter away, the entire time, nervous, "I still can't believe they planned everything for it to be here in New York. I'm so blessed to be a part of your family."

We eventually make it to the double glass doors, leading into the room full of my future. I turn towards Konstantin, overcome with emotions, "Thank you for everything, Papa!" I hug him again, squeezing him tightly. I love this man; he's been very good to me and my sister, and he doesn't even know her. I finally gave in and made him happy by calling him Papa about two months ago. He was so happy I looked to him 'like a father' he tried to send me and Tate to Fiji. I told him no way, but we'd definitely go to Fiji for our honeymoon!

Tate

My breathing stops when I see her. I gasp, at the beauty walking toward me, on what is fast becoming the happiest day of my life. With each small step she takes, I think of how lucky I am. Emily's absolutely breathtaking, resembling an angel. I can't believe in a few short moments she will finally be my wife.

Our path was stressful but to know we made it this far and love each other so much makes it worth it. I would do it again in a heartbeat. I would do it five different times if I had to.

This woman is my heart and soul and I would do anything for her. I never believed I could find a woman who would accept me for all my flaws. I never thought I could have a great relationship while being so involved in my Russkaya Mafiya roots. Or that I would find a woman to stand beside me and look forward to our future together.

Emily steps to the altar, and while I gaze in her sparkling green eyes, all I can think of is that this woman is finally mine.

Cameron, London and Cain? That's a story full of craziness, because guess what?

London has a SECRET. Hell, they all have SECRETS!

Warning- Book 2, Exposed- is full of action, witty remarks, fighting, torture, and steamy scenes with Mafia and MC Alpha men. It is NOT a love triangle, there is NO cheating in my books and everyone eventually gets their happily ever after. Thank you for reading and please consider leaving a review. - Sapphire

Thank you and I hope you enjoyed Secrets!

Acknowledgements

My husband – This life wouldn't be possible without having your continued support. I know it's not always easy when I zone out on my laptop and don't want to be disturbed. I appreciate you rolling with it and embracing my chosen career. I'm glad you've discovered a way to implement Knight Creations business to fit so well with mine. I wouldn't want to spend my life with anyone else. I love you, and I'm thankful for you. I can't say it enough.

My boys – You're my whole world. I love you both. This never changes, and you better not be reading these books until you're thirty and tell yourself your momma did not write them! I can never express how grateful I am for your support. You are quick to tell me that my career makes you proud, that I make you proud. As far as mom wins go, that one takes the cake. I love you with every beat of my heart, and I will forever.

My Beta Babes –This wouldn't be possible without you always being there to cheer me on. I can't express my gratitude enough for each of you. I'm blessed to have your continued support. Thank you.

Editor Mitzi Carroll – Your hard work makes mine stand out, and I'm so grateful! Thank you for pouring tons of hours into my passion and being so wonderful to me. Thank you for your amazing support and always being there whenever I need you.

My Blogger Friends – YOU ARE AMAZING! No, really, you are. You take a new chance on me with each book and in return, share my passion with the world. You never truly get enough credit, and I'm forever grateful! There are so many of you that have stuck with me from the beginning. That dedication is truly humbling.

My Readers – I love you. You make my life possible, thank you. I can't wait to meet many of you this year and in the future. To those of you leaving me the awesome spoiler free reviews, you motivate me to keep writing. For that, I will forever be grateful, as this is my passion in life.

And as always, ADOPT DON'T SHOP! Save a life today and adopt from a rescue or your local animal shelter. #ProudDobermanMom

Also by Sapphire

Oath Keepers MC Series
Secrets
Exposed
Relinquish
Forsaken Control
Friction
Princess
Sweet Surrender – free short story
Love and Obey – free short story
Daydream
Baby
Chevelle
Cherry
Heathen

Russkaya Mafiya Series
Secrets
Corrupted
Corrupted Counterparts – free short story
Unwanted Sacrifices
Undercover Intentions

Dirty Down South Series
Freight Train
3 Times the Heat
2 Times the Bliss

Complete Standalones
Gangster
Unexpected Forfeit

The Main Event – free short story
Oath Keepers MC Collection
Russian Roulette
Tease – Short Story Collection
Oath Keepers MC Hybrid Collection
Vendetti
Viking - free newsletter short story

Capo Dei Capi Vendetti Duet
The Vendetti Empire - part 1
The Vendetti Queen - part 2
The Vendetti Seven (Coming Soon)

Harvard Academy Elite Duet
Little White Lies
Ugly Dark Truth

Royal Bastards MC TEXAS
Bastard

Kings of Carnage MC Series
Bash – Vice President

Stay up to date with Wall Street Journal and USA Today Bestselling Author Sapphire Knight:

Website

www.authorsapphireknight.com

Newsletter

bit.ly/SKnightNewsletter

Facebook

www.facebook.com/AuthorSapphireKnight

BookBub

www.bookbub.com/profile/sapphire-knight

Instagram:

http://instagram.com/authorsapphireknight

www.ingramcontent.com/pod-product-compliance
Lightning Source LLC
Chambersburg PA
CBHW072056170626
46813CB00004B/1376